In The Shadow Of Gray Tower

for Jean
Enjoy
Nancy W. Collins

by
Nancy W. Collins

Portrait restored by Brian R. Dierberger
Gillard Photography, Fortuna California

IN THE SHADOW OF GRAY TOWER
This is a work of fiction. All characters and events portrayed in this book are fictional. Any resemblance to real people or incidents is purely coincidental.

First edition.

Library of Congress Preassigned card number program data
Collins, Nancy W.
In The Shadow of Gray Tower

Library of Congress Catalog Card Number: 99-94602

ISBN 0-9669515-0-6

Published 1999 by Nancy W. Collins

Printed by Eureka Printing Company, Inc.
Eureka, California

For my grandchildren

Preface

Janie's portrait hung on the living room wall, a small oil painting next to the massive, gilt framed pictures of her father's ancestors. On canvas, she is young and pretty with delicate features and brown curls falling gently to creamy white shoulders.

"It's not me," she insisted. "I did pose for that picture. It was designed to imitate those ancestors. Father thought I looked like his great grandmother or maybe his sister Grace who died of tuberculosis long ago. I don't belong in a gilt frame. I'm a plain girl."

You be the judge. This is her story.

Chapter 1

My eyes almost popped when I first saw Gray Tower. Sitting on top of a steep hill, it was built of dark stone with a tall tower in front and an iron balcony overlooking a manicured lawn and garden. At the age of eight, I'd never lived in a house like that before.

We moved into Gray Tower during the Great Depression. My family came from Florida where my father, Herb Brown, had managed several firms for a New York holding company. In 1937, it was heartbreaking work. He had to fire people in order to keep companies from going bankrupt. "If I fail, everyone will be unemployed," he explained to my mother, Rose.

The move symbolized success for my ambitious father. A short, powerful man whose dark hair was always neatly plastered down with hair tonic, he'd been made manager of the largest division his company owned.

I felt excited about moving. Father had told me that it snowed in Minnesota so I expected to see some when we arrived. I didn't know that it was hot in August. My fourteen year old brother, Sam, knew better. He laughed at me. "Silly Janie, you'll have to wait a long time before it will snow."

Our twelve year old bother, Don, nodded. He'd never seen snow either. He just always agreed with Sam. My brother's looked so much alike they could have been twins. Both were short and stocky like Father with unruly hair which kept falling in their eyes. Sam was taller and wore round, metallic framed glasses which made him look like an owl. Don had Mother's sapphire blue eyes though he lacked her delicate complexion and auburn hair.

I was plain, a bit overweight and awkward. Mother brushed my brown hair around her finger to make ringlets. It never stayed in place. The curls bounced about as I ran until I had a head full of snarls.

This new house frightened me. The front door opened into the round stone tower with an open staircase winding upward to the second floor. Those stairs seemed to be hanging in mid-air. An open landing circled inside the tower leading to two bedroom wings. Then an enclosed stairway circled again curving upward to a third floor tower room. At first, the climb scared me. What if I slipped between the iron railings and fell to the stone floor below?

Trembling, I crept up to the landing searching for my bedroom. I wandered from room to room until finally I saw the white double bed and rose-trimmed white dresser which had been my furniture in Florida. At last I'd found my room! Or had I?

A strange woman stood making the bed. She looked young and would have been pretty if she'd worn her blond hair down. Instead, she pulled it back in a stiff bun. Had my parents given this furniture to her, I wondered? She might be a maid. I wasn't sure. "Pardon me," I said politely, "I'm lost. Could you help me find my room?"

She laughed in a friendly way, then answered in an accent I could barely understand, "Yaa. I think this one is yours."

Oh thank you," I gasped in relief. I had found my room and met the maid, a young Scandinavian woman named Olga. She and her husband, Hans, would be our caretakers.

The servants seemed nice. But the house still worried me. Built on twenty acres of isolated farm land by an eccentric millionaire, it contained twenty six rooms and a large barn with a flight cage for pigeons.

The tower room had windows all around giving a spectacular view of the countryside. The only furniture in it was a round, felt covered table which, we were told, the previous owner had used for seances where people tried to contact their

2

dead relatives.

As an adult, I decided that Father bought Gray Tower because it reminded him of an European manor. His grandfather was an English knight. His father had not inherited the title. He'd come to America where he lived quietly as an accountant. Father was more ambitious. He had a temper, too. Sometimes in the night, I heard him yelling at Mother.

The house was so isolated that Father had to drive sixteen miles to work. Don and Sam could go to a boys' prep school a few miles from home. "Your school is in the city," Mother explained to me. "You will drive in with your father every day."

I nodded, then waited for an explanation. Mother was responsible for house and children. Looking like a porcelain doll, with sapphire blue eyes and auburn hair, everything she thought came out her mouth. She never considered other people's feelings. Most days, she spent reclining on a chaise lounge, sewing, and listening to soap operas on radio. When Father traveled, she went too. As an adult, she explained to me that Father believed himself to be an alcoholic. When he gave up drinking, he made Mother responsible for his sobriety. As long as she was with him, he didn't want to drink.

Mother also worried about her children upsetting Father. As a result, the boys and I handled our own difficulties.

Unfortunately, I had problems which I couldn't solve alone. In first grade, I learned to write left handed. In second, we moved to another school district where I was quarantined for months with whooping cough. When I finally returned to school, the teacher forced me to write with my right hand. By the time I reached third grade, I suffered from bronchial asthma and wrote upside down and backward.

This problem was compounded by the fact that I did not live up to Mother's idea of a daughter. Raised with two sisters, Mother believed girls should sit quietly playing with dolls or

3

doing needle point. I ran with the boys, playing ball or riding ponies. Mother wanted Shirley Temple. Instead she had a wild tomboy.

"We're sending you to private school," she continued. "They plan to put you back a grade. But they think they can teach you to write."

"I hope so." I dearly wanted to be like everyone else.

My new school required uniforms, so Mother took me to a dressmaker to be measured. In September, my uniforms arrived, plain blue cotton dresses. At least I will look like everyone else, I thought.

School started on a clear, cold September morning. "Hurry and eat your breakfast," Mother exclaimed. "Don't keep your father waiting."

"I'm trying," I answered stuffing corn flakes into my mouth. I had to force myself to eat. I had a big rock in my stomach.

"Let's go," Father called honking the horn.

Putting down my spoon, I rushed outside and climbed into his Cadillac. I enjoyed the ride. The cold air smelled of wood smoke and damp grass. We took a wide highway into town. My school turned out to be a large red brick building in an attractive residential area. Father stopped near the front steps. "Okay," he said. "This is it. When school is over wait on the steps and someone will pick you up. Look for this car."

"Aren't you coming in with me?" I asked, feeling sick to my stomach.

"No, I have to get to work. The school office is just inside that door. Go there and someone will show you to your classroom."

"All right." I had been to new schools before so I knew the routine. Climbing out of the car I started up a long set of stairs. Father waved to me before speeding away.

I joined other girls heading inside. The younger ones wore

uniforms like mine. The older girls wore light blue blouses, navy blue jumpers and black ties. They look like boys, I thought. I didn't have time to worry about it. A bell sounded and everyone started running. I ran, too, even though I didn't know exactly where I was going.

Father proved right. Just inside, an open door led to an office. There, I found a lady sitting at a desk. She had short gray hair and dark rimmed glasses which made her look stern, until she smiled at me. Her voice sounded kind. "You must be the new girl."

"Yes," I answered breathlessly.

"We must hurry, you're almost late," she explained taking my hand. We went down a long hall which smelled of floor polish and sweaty gym shoes. "This is your class," she said indicating a door. "The teacher's name is Miss Potter." She opened the door and waved me inside. There I saw ten girls seated around a large table. Oh boy, I am late, I thought feeling my face turn red with embarrassment.

"Hello," the teacher said smiling kindly. "Don't be afraid. Come in." She looked young and quite pretty. She had blond hair cut short. She wore a white blouse with lace around the neck and a pink cameo at her throat. "Girls," she announced, "this is our new girl, Jane." She pointed to an empty chair. "You can sit there."

As I sat down she put a tablet of lined paper in front of me. "We're practicing writing." She placed a pencil to the left of my paper. Thank goodness, I thought. She's going to let me do it my way.

This patient third grade teacher really did help me. She let me use my left hand, teaching me how to tilt my paper so the ink wouldn't smear. She had me practice the alphabet over and over until I stopped forming letters upside down. That'll show Mother, I thought. Someday maybe even Father will approve of me.

I still had problems. Mother couldn't understand left handedness. She tried to teach me to sew. Unfortunately, my stitches went in the wrong direction.

"You're hopeless," she finally declared.

Meals were even harder for me. Olga passed the food, holding each dish at my left shoulder. If I tried to serve myself with my left hand, I nearly broke my arm.

"Use your right hand," Mother insisted. "How often must I tell you?"

"I'm trying," I answered spilling vegetables on the tablecloth.

"You'll never get it right," Mother would declare. I did learn eventually. Now I can serve myself peas right handed without spilling one. I just take a smaller spoonful.

Father presided over dinner. He stood at one end of the table and carved. He loved roast beef so we had it often. While Father sliced the meat he told us stories, jokes or his political views. It was against his principals to swear unless quoting someone. He liked politics best. "That Roosevelt's an idiot." He waved the carving knife for emphasis. "He'll never be reelected. Those public works projects of his are bankrupting the country."

We nodded hungrily wishing he would hurry and pass us our plates. If Father dominated the dinner table, that tower dominated our house. A light switch controlled the chandelier. If you switched it once, all the bulbs lit. Switch it again and half of them went out. Under that light stood the round table. A previous owner had fallen on the hill and been killed. His widow tried to reach him with seances around that table.

Sometimes other lights went on by themselves or the doorbell rang for no reason. Our neighbors thought the house was haunted. Mother laughed at this. "It's only mice chewing on

6

the wires," she insisted.

One day, I sat playing outside the kitchen door when I saw a yellow cat coming up the walk. "Come look," I called to Olga. "I've found a beautiful cat."

"Poor thing," Olga said when she saw it, "she's half starved."

"Can you find something for her to eat?"

"Yaa. There are chicken scraps in the kitchen."

I sat on the ground and fed her one scrap at a time. Then I started petting her. Soon she was curled up in my lap purring contentedly.

"Can I keep her?" I asked Mother.

"Yes, I guess so. She can live in the barn."

"Thank you." I picked her up and carried her out. "Your name is Snook," I told her as I put her down.

It was a marvelous barn with three big box stalls for horses. Even so, when I first saw them I burst into tears.

Mother heard me crying as I came into the house. "What's wrong?"

"It's the barn." I wiped my eyes with the back of my sleeve. "It's so beautiful and now we don't have the ponies."

In Florida, we had owned two little Shetland ponies names Star and Larry. Father had bought them for my brothers. After the boys outgrew them, I had them all to myself. Larry was so gentle anyone could ride him. His brother, Star bucked and kicked. I didn't care. I loved them both.

Suddenly, as we were getting ready to move, they disappeared. Father had given them to a zoo. I couldn't believe it. How could I live without them? I cried and cried.

Mother explained that they would be better off in the zoo."It's a long way from Florida to Minnesota.They would have to ride in crates. They're getting pretty old, too . Your father knew they would be well cared for at the zoo."

"We're taking Pinky with us?"

7

"Yes, Pinky is a cocker spaniel. Dogs can ride in cars. Ponies can't." I had accepted it until I saw this beautiful barn. My heart hurt from wanting them.

"Can't we get them back?" I pleaded. I'll take care of them. I'll feed and water them every single day."

"No," Mother answered firmly. They belong to the zoo now." Sad and lonely, I spent my time playing with Snook in the empty barn. At least it smelled like ponies.

I had a hard time at school. All the other girls came from either the residential area nearby or they were bused in from a wealthy lake district. They all knew each other. I was an outsider. I lived in a totally different area with no one to play with after school.

The teacher often kept me late to work on my spelling which made me feel stupid. The school never gave grades so I always thought I was flunking.

I shut myself in my room at night and cried. "Please, God, give me back the ponies."

I wasn't unhappy all the time, of course. Minnesota was unusually beautiful that fall. Leaves turned crimson, squirrels carrying acorns chased each other up and down trees, and wild geese honked excitedly from every pond. The air smelled fresh and cold. Soon ice began to form. Ice! What fun for a child from Florida. I hunted for puddles after the first freezing rain. Then I stomped on them, watching ice crack under my weight. "When will it snow?" I asked Olga.

"Soon," she assured me. "I can smell it. There's snow in the air."

Finally one morning, I awoke to a glistening wonderland. It had snowed during the night and suddenly everything seemed beautiful. Even our strange house didn't look so terrible when covered with snow. The dark roof was now frosted with white and the huge evergreens next to the front door glistened in icy splendor.

I dressed as fast as I could and ran outside. Scooping up a handful of clean snow, I stuffed it in my mouth. It tasted cold, flat somehow. I had expected it to taste like ice cream.

"Put maple syrup on it," Olga suggested "That should be good."

"Okay." Taking a bowl from the kitchen, I filled it with snow and poured syrup over it. Then I had watery snow. It tasted sweet, but not good. "I guess you can't eat snow."

She nodded. "Maybe you'd better just look at it."

Disappointed, I wandered into the living room where I found Sam lying on his stomach in front of the fireplace reading a toy catalog. I sat beside him. The fire felt good on my cold face. "What are you doing?"

"Marking things I want for Christmas," he answered. "See, I'm putting my initials next to pictures of things I want." he shoved the catalog towards me. " Here, you can do it, too."

"I don't want toys. I want Star and Larry."

"Oh, stop it. You know the ponies are gone."

Later Mother said the same thing. "You can't have those ponies back, so pick something else for Christmas. How about a doll? Or a jewelry making kit?"

"All I want is the ponies," I answered stubbornly.

As Christmas approached, the pines in front of our house lay deep in snow. The oaks stood bare and frozen. I seldom saw squirrels now. Occasionally I found an empty corn cob under a tree. Somehow, they must have carried it from a nearby field.

Father bought a huge Christmas tree and put it up in the tower. Two stories high, it reached past the second floor landing, almost touching the chandelier. On it he placed glass ornaments the size of grapefruit. The tree was so big that we had trouble using the front door.

"Next year we will have a small tree in the living room like everybody else," Mother said.

Father only laughed.

On Christmas eve, Sam, Don and I pinned our socks to a rope which we tied across the fireplace. We hung up our stockings even though we didn't believe in Santa Claus.

Father sat in his easy chair and watched. "When I was a boy, all I got in my stocking was an apple, an orange and some nuts," he told us.

We nodded sympathetically without believing him.

"I hope I get a train in mine," Don declared.

"I don't care what's inside mine," I insisted. "Star and Larry won't fit in a stocking."

"Come on, Jane." Sam shook his head in disgust. "Be reasonable. You know you won't get the ponies."

Next morning, I awoke to Mother knocking on my bedroom door. "Time to get up," she called. "Hurry. We're waiting for you."

I jumped out of bed and stood shivering in the cold. Fumbling with my robe, I hurried downstairs. Mother met me at the bottom. "There's hot chocolate in the kitchen. Get some and come into the living room."

"Okay."

I saw Sam struggling sleepily down the stairs. Don followed him rubbing his eyes. In the living room, someone had rebuilt the fire, so the room felt warm. We children unpinned our stockings and sat down to open them. Mother and Father hovered nearby, watching.

Inside mine, I found a little doll with golden hair, a manicure kit and some hard candy. I put the stocking down and ate an orange drop.

"You're not finished," Father said. "There's something else."

"No there isn't." I held it up. "See it's empty"

"Look again. Put your hand way down inside."

I reached down into the toe and drew out a small piece of folded paper. "There's nothing. Just this."

"Read it."

Slowly, I unfolded the paper and read: *The ponies have been shipped. They will arrive on Tuesday.*

My heart leaped with joy. Now everything would be all right. I rushed over and hugged Father. "Oh thank you, thank you."

Pleased with himself, Father grinned. "You're welcome."

Having ponies made all the difference. My parents introduced me to Lea and Mimi Grosse, the daughters of Father's company doctor. They were close to my age and only lived three miles away. I rode over to their house almost every Saturday. I never followed the road. I cut through the woods, past corn fields and around fenced pastures filled with cows.

The girls went to public school because their father didn't think they needed an expensive education until junior high. Lea and Mimi were slender, with green eyes and hair so blond it looked like strands of sunlight. Lemon juice rinses kept it that color. They didn't know how to ride, so I taught them.

"It's easy," I explained. "Put your foot in the stirrup and swing your other leg over him."

"Here. Try it with Larry first. He's gentle." I held Larry while Lea mounted.

"Okay. Now what?"

"Hang on." I set off, leading Larry while Lea bounced up and down on his back. I knew nothing of riding technique. It didn't matter. Soon we were going for picnics in the woods carrying peanut butter sandwiches wrapped in wax paper and tied with string. We had fun. We couldn't go far because with only two ponies. One of us always had to walk.

One day the phone rang. "Come over quick," Lea said, her voice shaking with excitement.

"What is it?" I asked.

"I have to show you. Hurry."

Running to the barn, I saddled Larry and galloped over to their house. I found Lea and Mimi outside waiting for me. "Quick, to the pasture." Mimi jumped up and down with excitement.

There they showed me a little black pony. He snorted and pawed the ground when he saw us. Larry walked right up to him and touched noses. Friends already, I thought.

"His name's Pepper," Mimi said. She stroked his neck gently. "Isn't he beautiful?"

"Yes. He's a handsome pony." But why had their father only bought one, I wondered? He should have bought two. That would have cost too much, I decided. It didn't matter, now we had three ponies and could race through the woods at what seemed to us like breathtaking speed.

One Sunday morning in summer I headed for the Grosse's house, riding Larry and leading Star. As I rode through the woods near their house, I found a package tied to a tree branch. It was brightly wrapped like a PRESENT. Farther along, I saw another one. How strange I thought. I kicked Larry to make him go faster and galloped all the way to Grosse's house. There I found the girls in the barn brushing Pepper. "Come quick!" I shouted. "Come see what I found out in the woods."

"What?" Mimi asked.

"You have to see for yourself. Hurry."

"I'll saddle Pepper," said Lea.

Mimi jumped on Star and the three of us galloped off into the woods. "There!" I pointed to a package dangling from an oak tree.

Mimi screamed with delight. "A present! Is it for me?"

"I don't know," I answered. "I didn't put them there."

"Look." Lea pointed, "there's another one."

"I'm opening this one." Mimi pulled it out of the tree and tore it open. "It's perfume."

"Let's see if we can find more." Lea galloped around the woods.

"Okay," I agreed.

We searched the woods carefully and found twelve packages. "Let's take them home," Lea said. "I want to show my mother."

"I opened mine." Mimi held up the perfume, some nail polish and a lighter.

"I'm taking mine to my mother," Lea said.

"I will, too." I following her to their house.

The girls' mother was a plump, blond woman who never seemed to approve of me or the ponies. When she saw the packages, she frowned, "You can't keep these." She took them from us. "They belong to someone."

"Can't I keep just one? the perfume?" Mimi begged.

"No. I'm going to make some phone calls."

In a moment she came back. "Those packages belong to the Sharps next door. They're having a riding party. Their guests should have those gifts."

"Out in the woods?"

"The Sharps own that lot. They just let you children play in there."

"Oh." I could feel my face getting hot.

"Does that mean we have to take them back?" Mimi asked.

"No, I'll do it. You might break something."

"Thank you." I felt relieved, grateful that she hadn't asked me to do it.

Summer passed pleasantly. Then one morning in late August, as I rode Larry down our hill, I met a strange man coming toward me. He wore a big cowboy hat, and sat on a huge western saddle. What interested me most was his beautiful brown and white spotted horse. Even though I had never seen a cowboy except in the movies, I felt sure this must be one. He's lost, I thought, when he rode right up to me and smiled.

"Howdy. I'm looking for Gray Towers. Do you know where it is?"

"Yes. I live there."

"Good. You can show me the way. I've come to deliver this horse."

"What!" I exclaimed. I couldn't believe it.

"It's okay. He's a good horse. You want to show me your barn?"

"Yes, certainly," I stammered, still not believing it. I showed him the barn and the spare stall. He dismounted, led the horse inside, then removed the saddle. "Where do you want this?"

"We're getting the saddle, too?"

"You get everything."

"I guess you better put it over there." I pointed towards the saddle rack. I wasn't paying attention. I was admiring the horse.

"His name's Patches," the man said. "Find me a water bucket."

"They're are in the grain room," I answered showing him.

"Good. I'll throw him some hay, too. Don't feed him oats. They're too hot. Might make him sick in summer." He fed and watered the horse, gave him a final pat, then turned back to me. "I have to go up to the house and talk to your folks. You take good care of Patches."

"I will. I promise."

Alone, I unsaddled Larry and turned him into the pasture. I wanted to make friends with Patches. Taking a handful of hay, I held it between the bars of the stall. When he came close to eat it, I stroked his nose. It felt as soft as velvet. "Hello, Patches. I wish you could be mine."

Back at the house, I found Mother and asked her about the horse. "Your father bought him for the boys," she explained. "Don't you try to ride him. You're only nine and he's too much horse for you."

"All right," I promised. I didn't obey. Every time I went into the barn, I brought an apple or carrot for Patches. I talked to him or stroked his neck while he ate. "You want to be my horse, don't you, boy?"

Patch responded by snorting and rubbing his nose against my shoulder. He wants me to ride him, I thought. So one Saturday in late fall, I slipped on his bridle. I couldn't lift the huge western saddle which Sam used. Next to it I found a little English jumping saddle which had belonged to my grandfather. Perfect. Saddling Patches, I led him down the road, out of sight of the house.

"Easy boy," I whispered as I climbed onto his back.

Patches turned to look at me, snorted briefly and bucked me off.

"Oh, Patch." I picked myself up.

The horse stood still waiting for me, then nudged me gently with his nose.

"Okay, one more time." I climbed back onto his back.

Off I went again. Patch threw me five times. Finally, he decided to let me ride him. He never threw me again. We became best friends.

Sam and Don were more interested in girls now than horses, so Patches became mine. I rode him constantly. He seemed to sense my moods. When I felt happy, Patch carried me through the woods at lightning speed. If I was sad, he stood quietly beside me while I drenched his soft neck with my tears.

One morning I awoke to the sound of frantic cleaning. The vacuum roared and dishes clanged in the kitchen. What's going on, I wondered? It's Saturday. The house should be quiet. I climbed out of bed and headed towards the kitchen. At the bottom of the stairs, I found the hired man on hands and knees scrubbing the floor. "What's happening?" I asked sleepily.

"Big party tonight. Your mother wants everything cleaned." I nodded. Mother ran the house. In addition to the couple who lived in, she had a laundress named Anna who came twice a week. Anna sometimes helped out at parties. Mother usually spent her days traveling with Father or reclining on a chaise lounge in her bedroom.

Today, I found her in a steamy kitchen which smelled like shrimp. Mother had never fixed a meal. She only knew how to cook desserts. At Christmas time, she made mince pies and marvelously rich chocolate layer cake. Today she was baking lemon meringue pies and beautiful chocolate eclairs. My mouth watered and my empty stomach growled uncontrollably when I saw the eclairs. "Hurry and dress," she said to me. "I need your help."

"Doing what?" I took an eclair from a tray and stuffed it into my mouth. It tasted wonderful.

Mother turned and saw me chewing. "Leave the eclairs alone. There's cereal with bananas for your breakfast. When you've finished, you can fix the shrimp." She pointed to two huge kettles boiling on top of the stove.

I ate breakfast and dressed. Then, I peeled cooked shrimp, cut them down the back, and removed the intestine. It took me most of the morning. When I finished the shrimp, I prepared hors d'oeuvre. Little sausages, smoked ham and bits of cheese all had to be arranged on silver platters. I hated having to work when the boys didn't. I evened the score by swiping an eclair or an hors d'oeuvre every few minutes. In the meantime, the kitchen smelled wonderful as a huge rib roast cooked in one oven and fresh rolls in another.

"When the guests arrive," Mother explained, "you're to take the ladies upstairs so they can leave their wraps in my bedroom."

"Why can't you do that?"

"I'll be greeting people at the door. I'm counting on you to make the ladies welcome. If anyone asks for anything, you are to get it for them. Understand?"

"Yes."

"After everyone has arrived, you can help serve the hors d'oeuvres."

"Why can't Sam do that?"

"He's almost a man. Men don't serve food. He's taking Don to the movies."

" Why can't Anna do it? I want to go to the movies, too."

"I need both of you. There will be a lot of people."

I set my jaw angrily biting my tongue. " Sam and Don should help, too."

"You're a ten year old girl. It's time you learned how wives entertain their husband's guests. It's an important part of being a woman."

"I'd rather be a boy," I mumbled under my breath. I gave in finally. I put on my best dress, a navy blue silk with white collar and cuffs. I really looked nice in it. Only slightly fat.

The guests arrived on schedule. Mother greeted them at the door. She looked beautiful in a mauve silk formal. I marched up and down the stairs showing the women where to leave their things.

The men looked handsome in dinner jackets. Most of the women wore mink stoles over long evening gowns. One horrible blond woman came with dead foxes strung around her neck. They had little glass eyes which stared blindly at me. The woman patted me on the head. "What a nice BIG girl you are." She smiled sarcastically.

I hated her. I knew I was fat. She didn't have to tell me. "Thank you," I stammered escaping down the stairs.

"There you are," Mother said as I reached the first floor. "It's time to start serving. Go out in the kitchen and help Anna."

"Okay."

I found Anna in the butler's pantry filling a tray with glasses. She had changed clothes, too. She looked very professional in a new black dress with a white apron and a funny little white cap. Anna had never worn a uniform before, so I was surprised. "You look great."

"Thanks. Here help me."

"What do you want me to do?"

"I'm going to pass these drinks." she explained. "You follow me with a tray of hors d'oeuvres."

"All right." I put a small sandwich into my mouth.

"Stop that," Anna cried. "Those are for guests."

I laughed smugly.

Following Anna proved easy. She moved around the living room offering drinks to groups of people. I followed with food. I knew some of the people. I saw Dr. and Mrs. Grosse standing near the fireplace talking to a tall young man. Mrs. Grosse smiled and waved at me. I smiled back. I couldn't wave because the tray was too heavy to hold in one hand.

Suddenly someone spoke behind me. "Say Jane, don't you have a cat?"

"Yes." I turned to face the awful blond woman who had insulted me.

"I hear that you have a beautiful cat. I would love to see her."

"She is pretty. She lives in the barn."

"Couldn't you bring her in for a minute? I really want to see her."

"Maybe." I didn't know what to do. Mother had told me to pass this food. She had also told me to get the guests anything they asked for. "All right. I'll try to find her."

I took the tray back to the kitchen and went out to the barn to look for her. "Here kitty, kitty, kitty," I called. She didn't come. Then I heard a sound and there she was in a corner with a newly caught mouse in her mouth. "Come on, Snook, someone wants to see you." I picked her up with the mouse still in her mouth and carried her up to the house.

Everything went all right until I walked into the living room. My cat wasn't used to people. When she saw all those guests, she dropped the mouse. It ran under the coffee table. Snook jumped from my arms and raced after it.

Women screamed. Some climbed on chairs. Others pulled their long dresses up above their knees. Mother stormed towards me. Fortunately, at that moment, Snook recaptured the mouse, so I grabbed them both and ran back to the barn.

Mother met me at the door when I returned. I had never seen her so angry. "What were you thinking?" she shouted.

"A woman asked to see my cat. You told me to give the guests whatever they wanted."

"Go to your room and don't come out again tonight."

"Yes, Ma'am." Boy, am I going to get it, I thought. This is the time Father will punish me. I waited, terrified. Nothing happened. Father stayed downstairs with his company. Eventually, I heard the guests moving into the dining room. I slipped downstairs and into the butlers pantry. There I ate leftover hors d'oeuvres for my dinner.

Several weeks later I found myself alone in the house. Father had taken my brothers to a father and son dinner at their school. The servants had the day off. Mother was playing bridge at the Grosses.

"Why can't I do anything fun?" I had complained to

19

Mother earlier.

"Because your school doesn't have a father and daughter dinner."

"I should be allowed to do something else."

"Maybe someday. Tonight you will be here alone. You're ten. That's old enough to stay by yourself for one evening."

I felt really frightened. What if a ghost should get me? Or kidnappers. I had been terrified by radio broadcasts of the Lindbergh baby's death in 1932. Mother had reassured me. "We're not rich enough for kidnappers."

"Feed Pinky," she reminded me as she walked out the door.

"I will." Pinky, our blond cocker spaniel, was the only animal allowed in the house. He slept on the back stairs near the kitchen. Tonight, I decided, he would sleep with me.

I ate a peanut butter sandwich for my supper, I found a flashlight. I rattled the cover of the cookie jar. Instantly, Pinky appeared. As soon as he had eaten, we climbed the circular stairs to my bedroom. Outside, a strong wind blew. I undressed quickly and climbed into bed. I pulled the blanket up around my ears. "Come on, Pinky," I coaxed him up onto the bed.

As I lay listening to the wind, I heard something else, a strange noise coming from below me. My house made a lot of strange noises. This one was particularly ominous. I put my arm around Pinky and drew him close.

There was something wrong in the basement, I thought. I have to go down and see what it is. Good, it stopped. No, there it was again. Finally, I climbed out of bed, took the flashlight and started downstairs. "Come on, Pinky."

Everything looked fine on the first floor. The basement always frightened me. Even so, I knew that I had to go there now. Shaking, I crept down. The noise came from behind a closed door at the end of the building. I had never seen that door open. I held my breath as I flung it wide. I saw a flight of steep stairs leading to a subbasement. At the bottom, a water pump worked busily. What relief! I slammed the door, ran back upstairs and jumped into bed. I fell asleep with my arm around Pinky.

Chapter 2

We spent part of each summer at a lake in Michigan. Mother had lived there as a girl and considered it her home, so Father bought a summer cottage nearby. Getting to it wasn't easy.

"When are we going to Michigan?" Mother asked one evening.

"About the fifteenth of July," Father answered.

"Can't we go sooner? I want to be there on the Fourth."

"No, I have a meeting in New York."

"You can arrange it."

He did, of course. Soon we were busy packing. Mother had a strange way of doing this. Instead of giving each of us a suitcase, she selected a different case for each kind of clothing. "Okay," she'd say, " everyone bring your shoes and put them in the shoe bag."

She had a bag for coats and a case for everyone's pajamas.

"Why can't I have a suitcase of my own?" Sam asked.

"I only want to take one on board ship. The rest can stay in the car."

"I can't sleep on a ship. I won't need pajamas."

"Put them in anyway."

On the morning we were to leave, Don and I were still eating when Father decided that it was time to go. "Everyone in the car," he called. He went out to his Cadillac to wait. Every few minutes he blew the horn.

"We're coming," Mother yelled.

I hadn't finished breakfast. I didn't really want it.

"Finish your food," Mother insisted. "It's a long trip. I don't want you getting hungry on the way."

"I'll try."

Father blew the horn again. My stomach knotted up into a tight ball. "I'm finished." I pushed my plate away.

In the car, Father and Sam took turns driving. It was a long, hard trip by car to Manitowoc, Wisconsin, then across Lake Michigan by ferry. This was not one of those little boats which carries autos across small bodies of water. No, these ferries carried trains. Each one could handle forty freight cars and a few automobiles.

It was very dark and foggy by the time we arrived at the dock. I could hear a fog horn moaning in the distance. Switch engines chugged noisily as they moved strings of freight cars around the dimly lit dock. A black monster of a ship lay anchored with its rear end raised like a giant mouth. As I watched, an engine backed up pushing a string of freight cars into the hold. Father drove right down next to the tracks and stopped. "Everybody out. This is our ship."

It was spooky. I thought I might be hit by a train. "How do we get on board?" I asked.

"You'll see." Father took my hand. "Bring the suitcase, Sam."

He led me down the side of the track to a wooden staircase next to the ship. Mother followed with Don while Sam trailed behind carrying our suitcase. The stairs were old with worn white paint. They led up to the deck of the ship. "Wait here," Father said when we reached the top. "I have to go and see the purser about our cabins."

Mother and Don sat down on deck chairs. Sam dropped the suitcase beside Mother and followed Father. I was thankful to be on the ship at last. I wanted to sleep. I couldn't do that yet, so I climbed up on the rail to watch them load the freights. Every time the engine pushed a string of cars into the hold, the ship tilted in that direction. There were four tracks which held ten freight cars each. When they were all loaded, a man drove our car on board.

Suddenly a whistle sounded. I jumped, startled. "What's that?"

23

"It's the five minute warning," explained Father who had just appeared. "It means we're almost ready to leave."

"Come on." He waved a handful of large bronze keys at us. "Our rooms are ready. Time to go to bed."

Father showed us our cabins, tiny rooms with two bunk beds, a wash bowl, a small fan and one round porthole. "You'll sleep with your Mother," he told me.

I had hoped for a room alone. Sam had one instead. Father took Don in the room with him. Mother distributed pajamas and toothbrushes from the overnight bag.

I climbed into the upper bunk and fell asleep. I didn't sleep long. I awoke to the terrible sound of someone pounding metal with a sledgehammer. I sat bolt upright in my cot. "Mother!"

"It's all right," Mother answered sleepily. "They're fastening down the freight cars. Go back to sleep."

"How can I sleep through that?"

"Try."

Finally the noise stopped and I fell into an exhausted sleep. It didn't last long. Soon the hammering began again.

"Now what?"

"They're releasing the freight cars so they can take them off. It's morning. We're almost in port. You'd better dress."

I opened my eyes and looked at her. She had her clothes on. "Okay."

A few moments later, the ship docked at Elberta, Michigan. Tired and hungry, we straggled off into a foggy dawn. The town was asleep, so we headed straight for our cottage. The house sat high on a sandy bluff. Painted driftwood gray, it looked as if it might have washed up during a bad storm. A flight of stairs led to the front door. Halfway up a builder had provided a landing and bench in case anyone needed rest.

"We have a good caretaker," Father said when he saw the

24

inside of the house. "He's turned the gas and water on."

Mother nodded. "The house is clean. The beds are made up and the wood boxes full."

"Check the refrigerator. I told him to buy a few groceries." Mother headed for the kitchen."There's coffee, milk, and some rolls."

"Good. You start the coffee. Sam can build a fire. You other children come with me." Father pointed to Don and I. "You can carry suitcases in."

As soon as the coffee boiled, we sat down to eat at a large table covered with a flowered oilcloth. I could hear the crackling sound of birch logs burning and smelled their pungent smoke. The house began to warm up. The inside walls of the cottage were unpainted boards with no insulation. There was no furnace either. The summers were often cold. We needed a fireplace. On either side of it stairs led up to two lofts. The boys slept in one. I slept in the other. Mother and Father had a room and bath on the ground floor. A fourth bedroom in the back sometimes served as servants' quarters.

My room was in front above the porch which overlooked the lake. Besides comfortable wicker chairs, the porch had a large swing suspended from the ceiling. Made of brown canvas and enclosed on three sides, it looked more like a tent than a swing. As small children, Don and I spent endless hours playing on it. This summer however, something happened which upset me, terribly.

One day, as I sat on the swing reading, two of Sam's friends, Tom and Jack, came over and started teasing me. It was a cold, foggy morning. I had put on my beautiful, new Angora sweater. At age eleven, my breasts had been expanding rapidly. This embarrassed me. Still, I thought I looked quite pretty until Tom pointed at me and laughed. "Hey, Sam, look at your sister. What a chest."

25

All three boys jeered at me. I felt my face getting hot and knew that it must be beet red. "Stop that," I screamed. Tears stung my eyes. "Leave me alone."

I ran upstairs and took off that sweater. I never wore it again. In fact, I seldom left my room that summer. I stayed upstairs reading, avoiding everyone.

Chapter 3

That fall, I awoke to a room full of sunshine. In the distance, I heard the sound of guns and knew that pheasant season had begun. I'm glad I don't hunt, I thought. Pheasants are too beautiful to kill. Lazily, I rolled over enjoying my bed. I heard voices coming from the kitchen and smelled bacon.

I felt hungry. I put on a robe and headed downstairs. I found Mother in the dining room. She seemed to be in an unusually happy mood. "Good morning. I've a surprise for you."

"A surprise?" I repeated sleepily.

"Yes. I've enrolled you in dancing class. I met the teacher at the Grosses."

"Dancing! I was so startled that my little heart almost stopped "I don't want to go."

"Of course you do. All girls want to learn to dance."

"Not this one."

"You're almost twelve now. It's time you started acting like a girl."

"Yes, Mother." The best way to handle Mother was to agree with her and then ignore everything she said.

I put the conversation out of my mind just as I had forgotten about the party dress which she bought for me the week before. I hadn't cared about it because I never went to parties anyway. So I was surprised when Mother came up to my room and handed me a large box. "Here, put this on. It's your new dress which was just delivered."

"I'll try it on later. I'm reading now."

"No, put it on now. You don't want to be late."

"What do you mean?"

"We're leaving for dancing school in half an hour."

"For dancing school?" I repeated, suddenly frightened.

"Yes. Now stop talking and get dressed."

My head spun. I thought I was going to throw up. "I think I'm coming down with the flu."

"Nonsense. You're fine. Put that dress on right now."

"Do I have a choice?"

"No!"

I didn't think I looked too bad when I saw myself in the mirror. I had wanted a white silk dress with tiers of lace on the skirt. Mother had refused to buy it. Instead she insisted on a plain pink taffeta. "The white makes you look fat," she told me. "You're getting taffeta."

Now she expected me to wear it in front of strange boys. I was terrified. How could I possibly dance with them? I can't, I thought. I'll faint. Then I'll die.

The class was held at a women's club near my school. Mother dropped me at the door. "Behave yourself. I'll be back for you at seven."

Shaking, I walked up the steps and into a big ballroom. Everything seemed to be brown. The floor was polished wood which looked slippery. The windows were hung with heavy brown satin drapes. Around the sides of the room were straight chairs with seats covered in the same fabric as the drapes. In one corner sat an old fashioned phonograph which would provide the music. About two dozen children stood about the room. I recognized a few of them. Most were strangers.

The teacher was a small bony woman with long gray hair pulled back into a pony tail. She wore a dark green dress which looked too big for her skinny frame. She blew a whistle to get our attention. "All right, children, line up against the walls. Boys on my left. Girls on my right"

I bolted for the ladies room. I wasn't alone. I found quite a few girls in there. After a few minutes the teacher came in and herded us all back to the dance floor. She demonstrated counting, "one and two and three and four."

I could do the steps as long as I did them alone. Then the teacher called, "all right, boys, choose your partners."

Nobody chose me, so the teacher rounded up a boy, who seemed to be as frightened as I was, and told him to dance with me. I kept tripping over his feet. "I'm sorry. I'm sorry," I mumbled feeling my palms grow wet with sweat. As soon as the music stopped, I dashed back into the ladies room.

There I found a freckled, red haired girl named Gigi whom I knew from school. She smiled when she saw me. "Hiding out, too?"

"Yes." I felt my face grow hot.

Gigi tossed her head back and laughed. "Horrible isn't it?"

Suddenly I liked Gigi. I grinned back at her. "It certainly is."

"Have you brought any money with you?"

"Yes. A couple of dollars in my coat pocket."

"Good. Let's sneak out of here. There's an ice cream parlor down the street. They make wonderful chocolate sundaes."

"I'd love to, but my mother's picking me up here."

"Don't worry, we'll be back before this is over. You can wait inside the door then walk out when you see her car. She'll never know the difference."

"You're right. Let's go."

We slipped into our coats and out a side door while our teacher was looking in the other direction. Hurrying down the front stairs, we walked over to the main street. Bright lights shone along the busy thoroughfare. About a block away I saw a candy store.

"They serve ice cream in back," Gigi explained.

Inside were little round tables with metal chairs upholstered in red-and-white striped satin. Along each wall were booths made of dark, polished wood. Two girls from school sat in one eating ice cream. They waved to Gigi as we approached. A tall, curly haired girl named Betty called, "come sit with us."

"Okay." Gigi slid into the booth. "We're playing hooky from dancing school. "Do you know Janie?"

"I've seen her at school," Betty answered. "Hello, Janie. Is this your first time here?"

"Yes. I live way out in the country."

"Then order the cold fudge sundae. The chocolate is so thick they have to scrape it off the spoon with a knife."

Her friend, a short girl with stringy hair and pimples whose name I didn't know nodded. "It's wonderful."

"Thanks, I will."

The waitress who took our orders soon came back with the biggest chocolate sundae that I'd ever seen. Betty proved right. Under a mountain of whipped cream, I found a big glob of semi sweet chocolate covering the ice cream. I took a big bite. "Best I've ever tasted."

Gigi laughed. "We knew you'd like it. "They serve sandwiches, too, and cute little French pastries."

Betty nodded. "Sometimes we come here for lunch on Saturday."

"Would you like to come with us?" Gigi asked.

"Oh, yes."

"Good. I'll invite you over to my house and then we'll come here."

"Oh, thanks." I was delighted.

"We'd better get back to dancing school," Gigi said. "It's getting late. Your mother'll be looking for you."

"Yes, let's hurry."

We paid for our food and rushed back to the women's club. We arrived just as the class ended. I stood in the shadows trying to catch my breath before Mother's car arrived.

"Good-bye," Gigi called as I rode away.

"Did you have a good time?" Mother asked.

"Oh, yes, I had a wonderful time." I didn't explain that the wonderful time was at an ice cream parlor, not at dancing school.

"There, you see? I knew you'd enjoy it."

"Yes, Mother," I answered smugly.

The classes seemed less frightening now that I had a friend. Gigi invited me to spend the night at her house the next Friday. On Saturday, we met Betty for lunch at the ice cream parlor. Afterwards, we went to a movie. What fun! I was finally getting to know some of the people from my school.

One night in the fall of 1941, Sam and Father sat at the dinner table planning a camping trip. I was jealous of the fact that Father took the boys someplace that he wouldn't take me. "Why can't I go too?"

"You're a girl. They don't go wilderness camping."

"Why not?"

"We're going to Canada. It'll be rough with only men in camp. I can't take a girl."

"Then I ought to be able to go someplace. I'm twelve. That's old enough to travel alone."

"Maybe you could visit your grandmother." Father glancing down the table at Mother.

She nodded. "I'll ask her."

"Oh boy, thanks."

"Your grandmother could meet you in Chicago," Father suggested. "You could take the train. Would you like that?"

I nodded. "When can I go?"

"Not until Christmas vacation, provided your grandmother agrees."

"Will you call her tonight? Please."

"All right. I'd like to talk to her anyway."

Grandmother lived in a small town called Battle Creek, Michigan which was near Chicago. She often took the train into the city to shop, so she agreed to meet me.

I was so excited that I could hardly sleep the night before. My first trip alone! What an adventure.

Mother drove me to the train. She bought me a first class ticket in the parlor car. It had individual armchairs which swiveled and little tables with ash trays. A porter dressed in a white coat would bring drink orders from the bar. I ordered a coke and settled back in my chair.

Most of the passengers were old men in business suits. They sat drinking or dozing. I was bored. I didn't care. I was on my own and headed for adventure.

Chicago was a huge town with skyscrapers everywhere. I would have been hopelessly lost if Grandmother hadn't met me. I had no trouble finding her, a tall, distinguished woman with gray hair curled tightly against her head. She wore a tailored suit which matched her hair. She stood waving at the gate as I got off the train.

"Hi, Granny," I shouted, waving back.

"Did you have any trouble getting here?"

"No. It was easy."

"Good. We'll take a cab to the hotel. You can leave your suitcase there and freshen up."

"Okay." I picked up my little overnight case and followed her through the crowded station.

"If you ever need a taxi in Chicago, don't try to hail one in the street. They won't stop for a woman."

"How do you get one?"

"Go to a hotel or restaurant. Ask the doorman to call one for you."

"Is that what we'll have to do now?"

"No. There's a cab stand at the depot. Taxis here will pick us up."

She was right. There were plenty of yellow cabs waiting in front of the station. One of the drivers took my suitcase and opened the door for us. Soon he was weaving through traffic on the way to our hotel.

"Is there anything special you'd like to do?" Granny asked.

"No. Whatever you want is okay with me."

"I thought we'd go to the theater tonight. Tomorrow we'll go shopping. How does that sound?"

"Wonderful." I grinned at her. Even though I didn't know my grandmother well, I liked her. She and her daughter were nothing alike. My mother never asked me what I wanted.She told me what we were going to do and assumed that I would like it.

"There's a new play I thought you might like. It's a comic mystery called *Arsenic and Old lace* . The trouble is that the only seats available are way down in front."

"That's okay." I thought it sounded terrific.

As it turned out, the play scared me to death. Our seats were in the front row. When the murderer climbed through a window onto a darkened stage, he was almost in my lap. I wanted to scream. That would have embarrassed Granny, so I held my breath until I almost fainted.

After the play, we took a cab back to our hotel. Granny had chosen a comfortable one near the department stores. Our room was high above the street away from traffic noise. As soon as we arrived, Granny ordered a late supper from room service. "Do you like Welsh Rabbit?"

"Oh, no. I couldn't eat a rabbit."

"It isn't really rabbit. It's a melted cheese sauce poured over toast."

"That sounds delicious."

It was. Granny drank a glass of beer with her food. I had milk. As soon as we finished eating, I undressed and climbed into bed. It had been a long day. "Good night, Granny. Thanks for a lovely time."

"You're welcome. Sleep well."

The next morning we went shopping. We must have walked through every store in Chicago. Granny looked at hats and gloves. She made me try on a pretty dress which didn't fit."It will soon," she predicted. "You've lost so much weight."

"Yes, I've been dieting."

"Good. But there'll be no dieting on this trip. We're on vacation."

She led me down a funny little crocked street. "You'll like this."

"What is it?"

"It's a French restaurant. We'll eat dinner here. I'll buy some pastries for you to eat on the train tomorrow, too."

We went into an elegant little restaurant with a crystal chandelier and lace tablecloths. I ordered chicken crepes and a strawberry tart. The food tasted wonderful. I hadn't realized how hungry I was. After we'd eaten, Granny helped me pick out some little, decorated pastries to take home. "Don't take the eclairs or Napoleons," she advised. "They have cream inside which could spoil. Choose the cakes. They'll travel better."

"Okay." I picked out half a dozen little squares with different colored icing and sugary flowers on top.

The next morning Granny took me to the train station in a cab. I held my suitcase in one hand and the box of cakes in the other.

In the station, I put my things down to give her a big hug. "It's been wonderful."

"I've enjoyed it, too. Maybe you can come again sometime."

"I'd like that."

Just then the whistle blew and the conductor shouted, "all aboard."

"Good bye, Granny," I called back as I ran for the train.

I made it just in time. The door closed behind me and the train began to move. I found my seat in the parlor car and put my things down. The car was almost empty. Probably because it's Sunday, I thought. I had nothing to do except sit and look out the window. I didn't care. I'd had fun. The train rocked gently from side to side. The noise of the engine became monotonous.

I must have slept. Suddenly I became aware of someone standing beside my chair. Opening my eyes, I saw a handsome, young soldier looking at me. He was tall and blond with the biggest blue eyes that I'd ever seen.

"Hi, beautiful," he said. "Sorry I woke you."

"That's okay. Are you in this car?"

"No. I just walked back from the coaches to see what it was like."

"It's boring."

"Want some company?"

"Sure. Sit down." I felt my face getting hot. I waved at an empty chair. I'd never talked to a boy before. I had spoken to my brother's friends, of course. This was different. A boy actually WANTED to talk to me.

"My name's Carl."

"Mine's Janie."

"Where you headed?" He swiveled a chair around until it faced mine.

"Minnesota. I'm going home."

"Me, too. I've got leave for Christmas."

"Where do you live?"

"In Brainerd. My family's driving down to meet me in Minneapolis. I can hardly wait to see them."

"Have you been away long?"

"Too long. Say, would you like a coke?"

"Sure. Thank you. Maybe you'd like a pastry?" I open the

pink box and offered him a cake.

"No thanks. Let's go to the club car."

It was hard walking. The train kept swinging from side to side, causing us to bump into people's seats as we passed. The doors between the cars were heavy. Carl went first and held each one for me.

When we arrived in the club car, we found everyone clustered around the bar. They seemed very quiet and serious.

"That's odd," Carl said. "People are usually sitting at tables. Talking."

"You're right. Let's see what's happening."

Carl walked up to the bar and found a waiter. "What's going on?"

"Everyone is listening to the radio."

"Why?"

"Because the Japs just bombed Pearl Harbor."

"Oh, my God." He shook his head. "I have to get to my outfit."

I didn't understand. I had never heard of Pearl Harbor. I had no idea what the bombing meant. Carl knew. He caught the next train back.

Mother met me at the depot and drove me home. Everything seemed normal. I didn't know that nothing in my world would ever be the same.

In winter of 1942, Father gave the company chauffeur a new job in maintenance. This meant that I was allowed to ride streetcars home from school.

During the winter, Mother met me at the end of the line. She drove me the last three miles home. I enjoyed riding the noisy, yellow cars which ran on tracks throughout the city. They gave me a new sense of freedom. I felt suspended in time between the rigid discipline of school and Mother's authority at home. For a little while, I was my own boss.

On Saturdays, I sometimes rode the streetcar into the city where I met Gigi or Betty and saw a movie. We saw newsreels full of battle scenes. The war still seemed remote to me. It appeared very serious to Father. He had been an officer during World War I. Now he wore a major's uniform and trained with the national guard. In summer, he even spent two weeks at an army camp with them.

One day in spring of 1943, the farmer who lived down below us arrived with his horses and plow. I saw him coming and ran to meet him. "What are you doing?"

"Your father hired me to dig up your yard near the orchard. He wants to make a garden. After I plow, I'll empty the manure bin and work that into the soil. It makes good fertilizer."

"We're going to grow vegetables," Father explained that night at dinner. "A man from my office wants a victory garden. He has no space for one, so he'll plant this one. We'll share the vegetables."

The garden grew so well that we shared vegetables with everyone we knew. We ate everything except soy beans which tasted terrible. Father had read that soy beans were high in protein. They could be substituted for meat which would soon be rationed. None of us would eat them, so the next spring Father bought an incubator and fertile chicken eggs. An old chicken house in the pasture soon filled with wonderful yellow chicks. We fed them chicken mash, vegetable scraps and soybeans.

"Can I play with the baby chicks Father?" I asked.

"Yes. But don't become too fond of them. They're not pets. We're raising them for food."

Baby chicks are cute. Adult chickens weren't much fun. I soon lost interest in them. In the fall, a man came with a truck and took them all away. Father had arranged to rent a frozen food locker. He had the chickens dressed and frozen. We ate roast chicken all winter long.

Meat, sugar, butter, coffee and gasoline were rationed. We had little books with coupons which had to be surrendered whenever we bought these things. Father's work was classified as essential so he had all the gas he wanted. Mother and Sam had a limited number of ration stamps.

Mother decided I could walk home from the streetcar stop during good weather. I loved it. It cost ten cents to ride to the city limits and twelve cents more to my stop. If I got off one station earlier it only cost six cents more. By doing this, I could buy ice cream at a nearby drug store when I changed street-cars. By cutting through a golf course and around our lake, I made it home sooner. My dentist taught me this trick. He lived next door and rode the streetcar to save gas.

Meat became scarce. My school received meat coupons, because we were required to eat lunch there. People claimed that we received more meat than public school children who had to carry their lunches from home. Although this was true, we still didn't have much meat. We ate things like Spanish rice or spaghetti. My favorite school lunch was a whole head of cauliflower served on a huge platter with carrots and peas piled on either side and cheese sauce poured over everything.

During summer, we froze vegetables for winter. I helped in the kitchen. "Run out to the garden and get broccoli," Olga asked one hot August day.

"Okay." In the garden I found the man who shared it with us. He had just cut a mountain of broccoli. "Why do you grow so much?"

"Your father and I both ordered seed. He thought his brand would grow better. I thought mine would. We planted both."

I laughed. "Both kinds grew." I piled broccoli into a basket.

"Yes. We have too much."

I carried the basket in to Olga in the kitchen."Here's the

broccoli. What do we do now?"

"We wash it." She held a bunch under running water."See.You can do it."

"Okay. " I took a handful and held it under the faucet. "Hey, there are little green bugs in this stuff."

"Yes. You have to wash them out."

"I'll try." I spread the stalks apart trying to get water in between the budding heads. I wasn't very successful. I always thought we ate a lot of little bugs that winter. I kept quiet about it. At least they were the same color as the broccoli.

Olga put the washed vegetables into a strainer which she placed in boiling water for three minutes. This turned the broccoli bright green. Then she put it into bags for freezing.

Besides freezing vegetables, we stored carrots, potatoes, pumpkins and squash in sand in the root cellar. Olga made strawberry and grape jam as well as applesauce. We had plenty of stored food. Father had a man come to the house to make a barrel of sauerkraut. We never ate any. It exploded all over the cellar. What a horrible mess!

In summer of 1943, Sam joined the army. Before he left, he became engaged to a beautiful, auburn haired girl named Terry who wanted to be a dancer. My parents held a formal dance at our house to announce their engagement. It was a hot summer night with the smell of fresh cut hay in the air. I stood at the kitchen window watching the guests arrive. The girls looked elegant in lacy summer formals.Their dates wore tuxedos with white jackets. Our living room rug had been rolled up and soon a live band started to play.

I wore a short, linen dress and helped in the kitchen. I filled glasses with coke or seven up. Mother had ordered a case of each. Sam had wanted beer. "If we're old enough to fight, we're old enough to drink," he'd told Father.

"Not in my house. Not until you're twenty one."

Sam knew there was no point in arguing. He must have warned his friends. I saw people hiding bottles in our bushes.

Mother beamed as she watched the dancing. After a while she noticed quite a few girls standing around by themselves. "Why aren't those girls dancing?"

"I don't know. Ask Sam."

"I will." She went out onto the dance floor where Sam and Terry were dancing. "Where are all your friends?"

Sam stopped dancing and looked around. He and Terry were the only ones dancing. "I don't know. I'd better look upstairs."

Don's bedroom and bath had been set aside for the men, so that's where Sam headed. Curious, I followed him.

I found Don's bed heaped high with tuxedo jackets and heard laughter coming from the bathroom. Peeking in, I saw all the men kneeling around the bathtub. They were racing Don's little put- put boats. These were little tin boats with a chamber for water above a tiny candle. Heat from the candle created steam which was forced out through the back. It propelled the boat forward like a jet. The boats were wonderful fun. Unfortunately, Mother followed us upstairs. "Okay. That's enough of that. Everyone back downstairs."

"Ahhh," came the collective sigh.

The party broke up soon after and Sam left for the army a week later. I wasn't sorry to see him go. I played his phonograph records and read his books. It never occurred to me that he might not come back.

War still seemed remote to me. I was busy growing up. Fourteen and in ninth grade, I made the honor roll at school. I thought that Father would be proud of me. He never noticed. Like Gray Tower, Father cast a long shadow. Now president of his company, he traveled even more than he had before.

Lea and Mimi transferred to my school, so I had company

40

on the long streetcar ride home. In addition, I had a new friend named Jenny. She was an English girl who had come to live with her grandmother for the duration of the war. A small girl with dark curly hair and a wonderful, contagious laugh, she never spoke to me of the war in Europe or the bombs which ravaged her homeland.

She talked about American movies and loved to imitate John Wayne or Betty Davis. Then she would throw her head back and laugh as though she were the funniest thing alive. I had to laugh, too.

One spring day school ended early so Jenny and I walked down to a nearby park. We found a little pond with ducks swimming in it.

"Let's feed them," Jenny suggested.

"We haven't any bread."

"We'll pretend we have bread."

"How?"

"Watch." Jenny ran down to the water with her hand in her pocket. Then she carefully took out an imaginary piece of bread. Holding it out, she broke off nonexistent pieces and threw them into the water. Ducks crowded around quacking and flapping their wings.

Jenny jumped up and down with glee. "Silly ducks."

"You're sillier than the ducks." I laughed. "Now what'll we do?"

"This." Sitting down on the bank, she pulled off her shoes and socks and waded into the cold water.

"Look. I'm a duck." She flapped her arms like wings and ran up and down the beach. "Quack, quack, quack."

"You're crazy." I laughed until I choked."You make a terrible duck."

"You're right." She glided to a stop."I'm not a duck,I'm a lovely swan."

41

Although Jenny never spoke of her parents or the war, she did have a serious side. Sometimes after school, she walked with me to the streetcar stop. On the way, we visited Pete's Place, a little coffee shop run by an old man. I don't know how much business he had the rest of the day, but when we arrived the place was usually empty.

"Hello, Squeak," he'd say to me. "What'll you have?"

"Coffee and doughnuts."

Pete was a thin, scrawny man who wore a funny white hat and a tattered chef's coat which had to be at least two sizes too big for him. He knew what I wanted. It never changed. He asked anyway and he always called me Squeak.

"I call you that because you're shy as a mouse."

"She's not a bit shy," Jenny lied. "You should see her chase boys."

Pete chuckled as he poured our coffee. "We know who's doing the chasing, don't we Squeak?"

"Not me, that's for sure."

The old man fed us and joked with us. As Christmas approached, Jenny had an idea. "Let's buy him a present. We can give it to him on the last day of school before vacation."

"What could we get him? We don't know anything about him."

"How about a sweater? It's cold in his shop."

"We don't know his size."

"Okay. A scarf. Or maybe gloves?"

"Good. They don't have to fit perfectly."

On Saturday, we went shopping and found a scarf with matching gloves. They were a soft, gray wool and came in a pretty gift box. Jenny tied it up with a bright red ribbon. On the last day of school before vacation, we took it to him.

Jenny hid the box behind her back. She smiled smugly. "Hi."

Pete turned from the coffee urn he was cleaning. He looked tired. "Hello girls. No coffee today. I'm cleaning the pot."

"That's okay. We're not thirsty."

"We just came in to give you this." Jenny held out the present.

"What is it, Squeak? A joke?" His eyes seemed sad. "Are you girls playing a joke on an old man?"

"No!" I cried in horror. "It's a present. Really it is."

Jenny placed the box on the counter. "Please open it."

He picked it up slowly holding it away from his body. "All right," he sighed. " I'll go along with your joke."

He untied the ribbon and opened the box carefully as though he thought snakes would jump out. I held my breath, afraid he wouldn't like it.

Jenny jumped around excitedly. "Hurry."

I had never seen such a look of surprise. "They're nice," he whispered. He took one of the gloves from the box and held it against his cheek feeling it's softness.

"They're really for me?" Tears crept into his eyes.

"Of course." Jenny laughed with glee. "Put them on." Leaning over the counter, she tossed the scarf around his neck. "Now the gloves."

"No. Wait. Have some doughnuts." He fumbled for a plate and started piling doughnuts on it. "Free. Today they're free."

Jenny pulled me towards the door." No. We have to go. We're late."

"Merry Christmas," I cried as Jenny pushed me outside.

"Come back," the old man called after us.

We never saw him again. After vacation, I went back. The shop was closed. The old man gone.

Eventually the war ended. Sam returned to marry Terry and Jenny moved back to England. I missed her, but busied myself with other thing like school work and riding Patches.

One warm Indian summer day as I rode through the woods I came upon a strange looking structure hidden in a grove of willows. It was a hut made out of corn stalks. Someone had built a frame of willows and covered it with the stalks. In front, the ground had been cleared. A ring of stones contained the remains of a fire. As I stared at it, a boy appeared. He seemed about my age, tall and skinny with red hair.

"Hey, get away from there," he yelled. "That's my place."

"It is not. You don't own these woods."

"I own that shack. I built it. It's mine. I don't want any girls around, so get lost." He picked up a rock and waved it at me.

"I'm going, but I'll be back. You can't force me out." I turned Patches and galloped away. Anger boiled up in me. I had always had the woods to myself. I felt it belonged to me, my private place. This boy intruded. I'll show him, I thought. I'll come back at night and tear his shack apart. If he shows up, I'll let Patch trample him, gallop right over him. That will show him. I stopped. He was rather cute. Maybe I'd make friends. We could share shacks or picnics. .

It never happened. Winter arrived instead. Snow covered the fields. I forgot about him. Just before Thanksgiving, an invitation arrived from my friends Mimi and Lea who had grown into beautiful young ladies They were having a harvest dance. It would be formal.They had arranged a date for me. I shuddered at the thought.

"His name's Rob Howard," Lea said. "You'll like him. He has horses."

"I hate all boys. Besides, I'm a terrible dancer."

"You dance well enough. You're our best friend. You HAVE to come."

"All right. I'll do it. But only to please you."

Rob called me a few nights later. "Hello," a strange voice said, "my name's Rob. I've been asked to take you to the dance.

Will you come?"

"Yes, I'll come." His voice sounded nice, not sarcastic like my brothers' friends. "Are you picking me up? My house is hard to find."

"Mimi drew me a map. I'll be there. I'm supposed to ask what color dress you'll be wearing."

"It's blue." I only had one long dress.

"Light blue or dark blue. I have to know because of the flowers."

"Dark blue." He was going to bring me a corsage. Nobody had ever done that before. Maybe Lea was right. I might like him.

"Okay, I'll see you Saturday."

"I'll be waiting."

He brought me a gardenia. It smelled wonderful. Rob was kind of funny looking. His ears and feet seemed too big for the rest of him, as though he hadn't grown into them yet. He was fairly tall, brown haired and dressed in a new blue suit. He opened the car door for me.

The Grosse home looked lovely. Outside the front door a pile of bright orange pumpkins leaned against a stand of corn yellow stalks. Inside, the living room shown brightly with yellow and orange streamers. They had pushed the furniture back against the walls and rolled up the rug for dancing. At one end, a table held Thanksgiving delicacies, cold turkey and apple pie.

I had a wonderful time. When Rob danced with me, something amazing happened. We danced beautifully together. Gone was all the awkwardness of dancing school. We moved smoothly around the room. I loved it.

"Were you this good at dancing school?" Rob asked.

"No, terrible. I hid most of the time."

"So did I." He stopped for a moment and gave me a funny

look. I realized we were both remembering how shy we had been. The fear had vanished. We looked at each other for a moment, then burst out laughing.

Rob and I dated until we graduated from high school. He owned a beautiful Morgan mare. He loved her as much as I loved Patch. He let me ride her while he rode his brother's stallion.

One spring day we rode out into the meadow near his house. The air smelled of freshly cut hay. A warm sun felt good on our backs as we followed a deer path out through the fields, around a wood lot and up a grassy hill. Near the top, we found a small stream with a sandy beach. Deer tracks led down to the water. We stopped to let the horses drink.

"Let's rest a minute," Rob said.

"Okay." I jumped down and led my horse to the water.

"It's nice here. I could stay forever."

"Or at least until dinner time." I laughed as I sat down on the little beach. The sand felt warm. I lay back so I could feel its heat in my shoulders. I picked up a handful of sand and let it run between my fingers.

Rob sat beside me. Leaning over, he kissed me hard. "I love you."

"I love you, too." I answered lightly, thinking it a joke.

"I mean it. I really love you. I want to marry you."

"Marry me!" I jerked away. " I can't marry you. I want to go to college, travel, write. I'm not ready for marriage."

"You don't need those things. My dad will give me a job after graduation. We can stay like this forever."

"Let me think about it."

"Okay." Rob found the horses who had wandered down stream a little. As I mounted, I realized I would never marry Rob. He was nice, but boring.

Graduation came at last. My school had a big dance to

celebrate. Before the dance, I invited Rob to dinner at the country club. Lea and Mimi invited their dates too, making a table of six.

"What color dress are you wearing this time?" Rob asked.

"It's plaid." I had bought an old fashioned dress of brown yellow and white.

"What kind of flowers go with plaid?" Rob sounded bewildered.

"I don't care. Anything will do."

"I'll ask my friend, Jack. His father's a florist."

On the day of the dance, a huge box arrived. Inside, I found a corsage about a foot long. It contained every kind of flower imaginable.

"What beautiful flowers," Mother lied when she saw them.

"They're a joke."

"No, they're not. Rob sent them. You have to wear them."

"Mother, he's teasing me. They're supposed to be funny."

"When a boy spends his money on flowers, you have to wear them."

"Okay, if you say so." That evening I pinned the flowers on my dress. They reached from my shoulder to my waist. I looked like a walking bush when I answered the door. "Hi, Rob"

"Hello." He stood and stared at me. "You look marvelous."

"Thank you."

When we reached the car, he handed me another florist box. "Take those flowers off. You weren't supposed to WEAR them. They're a joke."

"Mother said that when a person gives you flowers you have to wear them, so I am." I had thought of a way to put the joke on him.

"Here." He thrust the other box into my hands. "Open this."

Inside, I found a beautiful spray of tiny brown orchids.

"They're beautiful, but I'm wearing the ones I have on." I couldn't let him off the hook that easily.

I wore those flowers all through dinner. Everyone at the country club stared at me. Rob nearly died of embarrassment .On the way to the dance, I took them off and put on the other corsage. "These orchids are beautiful.Thank you."

"You're welcome. But it's the last time I play a practical joke on you."

"Good." I had a wonderful time at the dance. Afterward we drove to an open house, then out to breakfast. The sun was rising when Rob brought me home. I could smell apple blossoms in the fresh morning air.

"I'm going riding," I told Mother who heard me come in.

"No, you're not. You're going to bed."

"I'm not sleepy."

"Bed," she commanded, pointing towards the stairs.

I fell asleep thinking of orchids and apple blossoms.

Chapter 4

In September of 1947, I left for college in Colorado. "You change trains in Omaha," Father told me. "That's where you catch the express from Chicago. There will be other students on that train. You might meet some of them."

Father had bought me a first class ticket and a compartment out of Omaha. "I'm giving you a round trip ticket, because you're a girl," he explained. "Your brothers had to buy their return tickets out of their allowance."

I didn't argue. At age eighteen, I was excited about going. College meant really being on my own. My high school had prepared me for a fancy, eastern girl's college. I hadn't wanted that. I picked a small co-educational college out west. I wasn't competitive enough for Ivy league.

On the train out of Omaha, I found my compartment, stuffed my suitcase under the seat and sat down. As the train pulled out of Omaha I heard laughter coming from the next compartment. I opened my door and peeked out. The door next to mine stood open. Inside, two girls and a young man sat eating lunch.

I stuck my head around the corner and smiled at them. "Hello. Are you on your way to college ?"

"Yes," one of the girls answered. "We're going to Colorado."

"We're freshmen," the other added.

"So am I."

"Come on in," the boy invited. "The more the merrier."

I squeezed into their little room. "My name's Jane."

"Hi. I'm Patrick Haines"

He was short like me with sandy hair and a wonderful smile. "These girls are Sally and Connie from Chicago."

The girls looked enough alike to be sisters. Their dark hair was cut in identical bobs. They both wore cardigan sweaters with plaid skirts.

I nodded 'hello.'

"We're trying to eat lunch," Patrick explained. "This table is so small. Every time the train jerks, a plate falls into one of our laps."

"See." Sally pointed at the floor. "Wall to wall French fries."

I laughed. "What you need is more space. These compartments are too little for three people."

"They open up," Patrick explained. "We could ask the porter to fold back the wall between this room and yours. Then we'd have enough room."

"Okay. That would be fun."

Patrick rang for the porter. He shook his head when he heard what we wanted. "I can't open the door between a man's room and a woman's."

"It's not my room," Patrick told him. "I have a berth in the next car. This compartment belongs to these girls."

"Please open the connecting door," Sally pleaded.

"All right. If you young ladies want it."

Connie and I nodded. Opening that door made the room much larger. The four of us spent the rest of the day together. When night came, the porter told Pat to leave. He made up three berths for Sally, Connie and me. Climbing into mine, I wrote to Rob before falling asleep. It had been an exciting day. I slept well despite the clanging and jerking of the train.

At college, Connie, Sally and I found that we were all housed in the same freshman dormitory. It held fifty girls. I had a single room on the second floor. A few upper class girls shared the building with us, but most of us were freshmen. We could come and go whenever we wanted during the day. At night, we had to sign out. Then we had to sign back in when we returned.

They locked the doors at 10:OO PM on week nights and at midnight on weekends. After hours, you had to ring a bell to get in. They counted the time you were late. If you accumulated seven late minutes, they "roomed" you. This meant that you couldn't leave the building for one evening. People who were roomed for more than two consecutive nights climbed down the fire escape.

The first week I had a jumble of meetings and parties, but no classes. I registered, opened a checking account with a cashier's check which Father had given me, and stood in line at the bookstore. I went to parties which sororities held for us. I wore all three of the cocktail dresses which I had brought with me.

On Saturday, the school held a western cookout and bonfire. The smell of sage mingled with smoke in the clear mountain air. After dinner a band played country music. As I sat watching the flames, Pat appeared and sat beside me.

"How's it going?"

"Fine. Exciting."

"A fraternity has invited me to a dance next Saturday. Do you want to go?"

My heart jumped. I liked Pat. He made me laugh. "I'd love to."

"Good." He reached over and put his arm around me. We sat close together listening to music and watching the flames from the bonfire. His arm felt good around me. I knew I would be happy here.

The next morning I slept through Sunday breakfast, so I headed for a nearby coffee shop. Inside, I saw Pat sitting in a booth with a big, blond man. He looked like a football player.

"Hi," Pat called. "Come meet my roommate."

I walked over, happy to see him again. "Good morning."

"This is Hank."

"Hi, Hank. I'm Jane."

Hank smiled. "Glad to meet you. Want to sit with us?"

"Sure." I slid into the booth. "Are you a freshman, too?"

"Yes. I'm from upstate New York. This is my first semester."

"Have you registered yet?"

"Yes. They certainly don't give freshmen many choices. Science is about the only elective."

"We can take biology, chemistry or geology," Pat added. " Which did you choose?"

"I'm chemistry," Hank added.

"I'm chemistry, too." I said. "Maybe I'll see you in class."

"Why would a girl take chemistry?" Pat asked. "I thought girls always studied biology like me.

"I'm allergic to formaldehyde," I explained. "In high school, every time I tried to dissect something, my eyes watered until I couldn't see."

"You cried your way through biology?"

"It was pathetic. Finally the teacher let me use her sink. I kept my specimens under water."

"Did that work?"

"Yes. But I don't want to do it again. I'm taking chemistry."

Hank nodded. "I'll watch for you."

"And I'll see you Saturday night," Pat added.

"I'm looking forward to it." I meant it. I really liked Pat.

The first week of school proved hectic. Just finding the right buildings seemed hard. All the classes in my small high school had been held in one building. I wasn't used to walking around a large campus. Here they held literature in one building, science in another.

I slept soundly at night. Pat filled my dreams. Pat smiling. Pat laughing. Pat holding my hand. I still wrote Rob every day. Lying. Telling him I missed him when I really didn't miss him or Gray Tower at all.

Saturday night came at last. Pat arrived promptly at 8:00PM. He looked handsome in a gray suit and stripped tie. I hadn't seen him dressed up before. Even his shoes were shined. I wore a pale lavender cocktail dress with a full skirt which made my waist look small.

As we walked across campus Pat took my hand. It was a warm night, a large harvest moon hung in the sky. The air smelled of fresh cut grass with just a hint of sage brush. Stopping in the shadow of a large pine tree, Pat pulled me close, kissing me hard. Something inside me jumped. Kissing Rob had never been like THAT! I realized I loved Pat.

"I want to go steady," Pat whispered. "Will you?"

"Yes." I had only known him a week, but it felt right. I had never been happier. I hardly remember the rest of that night. We danced. We laughed. We walked home in the moonlight. Pat found a dark spot in the shadows around the side of my dorm. He pulled me close, kissing me again and again. "I love you."

"I love you, too," I answered meaning it. I didn't want to leave him. Eventually I pulled away. "I have to go in. They'll lock me out soon."

"I know. I'll call you tomorrow."

"Good night, Pat. I love you." I ran for the door making it just in time.

The college was full of men. After the war, Congress passed the G.I. Bill which paid college expenses for returning veterans. My school had ten men for each woman student. Many of them were quite old. Chemistry class was a good example. I opened the door to my lab class and stared in dismay at a room full of strange men. I was the only female. The professor had assigned places in alphabetical order. "The person next to you will be your partner," he explained. "You'll work together as a team."

Our first assignment involved heating a piece of glass tubing, bending it to a 90 degree angle. Then inserting it in the top of a cork. The man who was supposed to be my partner was busily trying to bend his stirring rod. I panicked. He's so much older than I am, I thought. He'll never listen to me. We'll both flunk. Half way down the room I saw Pat's roommate. "Hank," I cried, "will you be my partner?"

"Sure, why not."

I moved my equipment down beside him. The teacher didn't care. Neither did the other students. They simply regrouped and went on working. I felt better. Hank knew the difference between glass tubing and a stirring rod.

School went well. The work seemed easier than high school, but with more distractions. Pat and I joined fraternities. We had meetings and parties every week. Girls in this school didn't live in their fraternity houses. I continued to room at the dorm.

Time went quickly. Before I knew it, Christmas vacation arrived.

"Are you taking the train home?" Pat asked.

"Yes, I have another compartment."

"Good. We'll throw a party."

"Okay." I was wrong. I developed a flaming sore throat. I could hardly swallow. Eating was out of the question. I discovered that drinking grapefruit juice would numb my throat for several hours. I drank it even though it burned like crazy going down. I didn't want to go to the infirmary. The doctor would put me to bed. I'd miss exams. That would have meant staying at school to take make up tests. I didn't want to do that, so I drank grapefruit juice. When I finished my last test, I headed for the infirmary.

"Sit down," a nurse said as she put a thermometer in my mouth. After a few minutes she read it. "You have a temperature of 104 degrees."

The doctor looked down my throat. "That's strep throat. I'll give you a shot of penicillin and keep you here in bed for a few days."

"No. Please don't do that. I'm supposed to go home tomorrow."

"On the train?"

"Yes. I have a compartment."

" Will you stay in bed on the train and see your doctor at home?"

"I promise."

"Okay. I'll give you the shot and you can go."

I felt terrible. I fell into my compartment on the train. Soon Pat arrived with an assortment of friends. "Ready to party?"

"No. I feel awful. I'm sick."

"I have a roomette in the next car It's too small for a party,but perfect for   sleeping."

"I'll trade you."

"Done." Pat moved my suitcases into the roomette. I collapsed into bed. During the night, my fever broke. I awoke weak and terribly thirsty. When I tried to get a cup of water to my mouth, my hand shook so hard that I spilled most of it. The rocking of the train made matters worse. It took four tries before I managed to quench my thirst. The transfer in Omaha went easily. I dozed in my seat all the way home. Father's chauffeur, reinstated now that the war was over, met me at the station and drove me home.

"You look terrible," Mother said as I walked in the door.

"I've got a strep throat."

"Why didn't you take care of yourself? I'll have to call Dr. Grosse before you give it to everyone and ruin Christmas."

"Sorry, Mother." I dropped my suitcases in the hall and headed upstairs. I drank a huge glass of water and climbed into bed. I fell asleep almost instantly. I awoke to find Dr. Grosse was standing beside the bed holding a thermometer. He took my temperature, then examined me. "What treatment have you had for that throat?"

"Penicillin at the school infirmary."

"Good. I'll give you another shot of it. That should take care of you."

It took care of me all right. I broke out in huge hives. When Rob called I refused to see him.

"Why can't I come over?" he asked over the phone.

"I feel terrible and I look worse. I can't see anyone."

"But I love you. I don't care how you look."

"I care. I'm going to sit in my room and scratch myself silly."

"Can't the doctor give you something for the itch."

"He said to put ice on it."

"I'll bring some over."

"No. Don't come." I wanted to break up with him so I added, "I think you should start dating other girls."

"What are you talking about?"

"I don't want to go steady anymore."

"Are you trying to tell me that you've found someone else?"

"I'm sorry, Rob." I really did feel bad about it.

"I guess I understand. If you ever change your mind."

"Thanks, Rob. We'll still be friends."

"Friends it is."

"Bye, Rob."

It sleeted most of Christmas week. I stayed in my room, sick and miserable .On my last day at home, both the weather and my spots cleared up. I hurried down to the barn to check on the horses. Star and Larry were fine. I found them scampering around the pasture. But something was terribly wrong with Patches. He lay in his stall with one leg stretched out in front of him. Patch never did that!

"What's wrong, Patch?" I felt his leg and foot carefully. The hoof was burning hot. Bending his knee so the bottom of the hoof faced up, I saw a nail sticking out of the center."

"Oh, Patch."

My parents had hired new servants during my absence. The man was building himself a trailer in the pasture. Apparently he had scattered nails around on the ground and Patch had stepped on one. I was FURIOUS! Stupid man. He should have built his trailer on the other side of the barn away from your pasture.

I ran to the tool shed for pliers and disinfectant. "Easy boy, I'll take care of you." I pulled the nail from his foot, then poured a whole bottle of hydrogen peroxide into the wound. "That should fix it," I told him as I gently stroked his neck.

I hurried up to the house. "Where are my parents?" I asked the cook, a strange little woman who didn't act as if she had a brain in her head.

She shrugged. "Gone out."

"When will they be back?"

"Tonight, maybe."

"My horse is hurt. I've done what I can for him. If he isn't on his feet by this afternoon, he's going to need a vet."

She shook her head as though she didn't understand.

I tried to explain. "I have to leave for school this afternoon. I think Patch will be all right. If he isn't, you have to tell my parents right away. Do you understand?"

"You better write a note."

"All right. You make sure they read it as soon as they get home."

"Yes, okay."

I gave her the note. Then I went back and with another bottle of hydrogen peroxide and cleaned Patch foot again before dressing to leave. We never had a veterinarian. I didn't know anything else to do.

The chauffeur drove me to the train. Tears burned my eyes as we passes the barn. "Bye, Patch," I whispered. "I hope they take care of you."

Winter term passed quickly. Soon it was spring break. "Let's go skiing," Pat suggested. "My fraternity is sponsoring the trip. They're providing a bus and a chaperon."

"Okay," I agreed. "I don't ski well, but I'll try."

"You can use beginner's slopes. They're easy."

The bus took us to Winter Park, Colorado. It wound up the mountain into a beautiful, lacy wonderland. New snow had fallen during the night. It covered buildings and trees with a white, glittering meringue. We stopped next to a rustic frame building.

"All out," our chaperon called. She was the wife of an alumni and fraternity member who had accompanied us. They looked about twenty years old. Being married made them acceptable chaperons.

"This is the bunkhouse," her husband explained. "Girl's dorm to the left. Boy's to the right."

We picked up our gear and headed inside. The door opened into a large living room with overstuffed chairs, sofas and a huge fireplace. A fire crackled cheerfully on the hearth. I had never seen such huge logs.

"Oh, wow! " I cried. "Look at this."

"It's nice," Pat agreed. "We're going to have a blast."

"We might even ski."

"Let's look at the bedrooms."

"Okay." I headed left. The door at the end of the living room led into a large dorm full of bunk beds. There must have been at least twenty. In the middle stood a round, black, coal stove which glowed red hot. There were several girls milling around. I didn't recognize any of them. I saw our chaperon's wife, an athletic looking woman with sun glasses on top of her knit hat. "Put your things on a cot," she told me. "You'll be given blankets and a pillow later."

I picked out an upper bunk near the stove and put my small suitcase on it. Since I didn't know any of the other girls,I went back into the living room to find Pat. "I'm starved," he said as he came out of the men's dorm. "Let's go eat."

"Okay. I'll get my jacket."

The dry powder snow crunched noisily under our feet as we walked toward the cafeteria. This snow felt different from the wet, icy snow of Minnesota.

"It skies differently, too," Pat explained. "You have to keep your tips up or you'll plow right down into it."

"It's weird."

"You'll get used to it."

After a steak dinner we returned to the lodge. The wind had come up making it frigid outside. Inside it felt toasty. Pat found a big, overstuffed chair in a dark corner. "Let's sit here."

I nodded. We settled down close together. Pat put his arm around me. He kissed me gently. Somewhere music played. The fire flared, then died back. I felt happy and warm snuggled next to Pat. Nothing else mattered. I must have dozed until Pat moved waking me. "Time for bed. We've got a full day tomorrow."

"I'm ready."

He kissed me lightly on the forehead. "Sleep well."

"Night, Pat." I yawned and stumbled into the girl's dorm.Inside, it felt terribly cold. The stove no longer glowed red. Only a few embers remained. I found my cot by their faint light. On it were a pillow and two olive drab, down comforters. I guessed they must have been army surplus. I folded one in half and put it on the cot. I put the second one over it. I slipping out of my pants leaving my sweater and long underwear on. I crawled in under the second comforter and fell asleep almost instantly.

I awoke to the sound of someone lighting the stove. The comforter was pulled over my head with only my nose sticking out. It's too cold to get up, I decided. I lay there waiting for the room to warm up. Finally, I pulled on my pants and headed into the bathroom. Water in the sink had turned to ice. Fortunately, the toilet worked. I decided to put off washing.

Outside, our chaperons were loading everyone into our bus. "Hurry," Pat called. "We're going out for breakfast."

I pulled on my jacket and climbed aboard. Pat followed sitting beside me. "We're headed for a lumber camp. They have wonderful breakfasts."

"Good. I'm hungry."

A few minutes later we arrived at a rustic looking wooden building. It smelled of wood smoke and coffee. We paid a small fee for an all-you-can-eat country breakfast. We sat at long tables which were soon piled with plates of pancakes, platters of ham and eggs and huge bowls of fried potatoes. Large pitchers of syrup and a pot of coffee stood at each end of the tables. "I'll never get used to western breakfasts," I told Pat. "They're so big."

He laughed. "I love them. They give me plenty of energy to ski."

I ate a big breakfast which turned out to be fortunate. I needed all the strength I could muster. Skiing was such fun that I never wanted to stop.

On the last day, I decided to try something difficult. A new run had just been opened. I couldn't resist it. A warm sun shown brightly on the snow covered evergreens which glittered like diamonds. Snow lay deep in billowy drifts. Alone at the top of the world, I couldn't believe the quiet. A single pair of tracks stretched before me. Only one other person had skied this trail.

"What are you doing here?" an angry voice cracked from behind me.

Turning, I saw Pat getting off the tow. "You're not good enough to ski this hill.It's for experts."

"I couldn't resist. It's so beautiful up here."

"How will you get down?"

"I'll make it."

"I hope so. I'll follow you just in case."

"Okay. Here I go."

"Keep your tips up," Pat shouted.

It seemed easy at first, but soon I was flying faster and faster down the slope. A building appeared below me. I was headed straight for it.

"Turn," Pat screamed.

I panicked and tried to snow plow. I knew I couldn't do that in deep powder. I did it anyway.

****

"I'm putting you in the hospital," the strange, middle aged doctor explained. "You have a fractured cartilage in your knee. After a few days in traction, I'll be able to put a cast on it."

"I can't go to the hospital. I have classes."

"You're going to miss a few, but the cast and crutches, you'll be able to get around."

I sighed. "I guess I don't have much choice."

"No, you don't."

The accident didn't do my grades any good. I had to cross the campus on crutches three times every day. It was exhausting.

Although Pat still dated me, he didn't enjoy it. A girl in a cast isn't much fun. "I'll come and visit you next summer," he promised one day. "By that time you'll be well."

"I'll be in Michigan all summer, at the cottage."

"Good. It's closer to Chicago. I can drive up."

"Promise?"

"I'll come. You'll see."

I arrived home in June still limping. As soon as I reached the house, I hurried down to the barn to see Patch. The barn was empty!

I rushed back up to the house. I found Mother lying on her chaise lounge reading a magazine. "Where are the horses?"

"Your father gave Star and Larry to a neighbor down the road. He has young children to ride them. He said you could visit whenever you wished."

I nodded.

I wanted to scream, 'Where is Patches?' but I didn't. I already knew the answer. Anger boiled inside me. That idiot cook! There was nothing I could do. I turned and limped sadly away.

Chapter 5

Thank goodness for the cottage. There was nothing left for me at home. For the first time in my life, I felt happy about going to Michigan. We drove two cars. Father and Mother went first in the Cadillac. Don and I following in Mother's Buick. Father only planned to stay a few days. He would return in August for his vacation.

As soon as we finished unpacking, I walked down to the beach. It was deserted except for a group of girls playing bridge in their swimming suits, hoping to get a tan. I recognized one of them, a pretty girl with dark curly hair and freckles. Cybil lived a few cottages from me.

"Hi," she called to me . "When did you arrive?"

"This morning," I walked over to her.

"Good. You can come to auditions this afternoon."

"What auditions?"

"Her mother's directing a play called *January Thaw* at the community center," another girl explained. "We're all going to try out."

"You must come."

"I can't act."

"Doesn't matter. You can watch."

"Okay. I'll come. I need something to do."

The play was being put on by the Christian assembly. Cybil's mother taught college dramatics in winter. She had agreed to direct it.

After lunch, I walked through the woods to the rough, un-painted building which served as church, theater and meeting hall for the assembly. I found Cybil and other young people on stage reading lines.

As I sat down to watch, Cybil's mother saw me, "Would you hold the book?"

"How do I do that?"

"You read the script and prompt the actors when they forget their lines. You have to come to every rehearsal. Interested?"

"Sure. It'll be fun."

"Good." She handed me a copy of a play called *January Thaw.*

I sat down in front and watched. Cybil a college senior, played the lead. After the auditions, she introduced me to the cast. I knew nothing about dramatics.I was amazed by the way people changed as soon as they set foot on stage. They really became the characters.

I liked Rusty Smith best. A big boned man with reddish brown hair and a scar on his right cheek, he was a junior at M.I.T. One day, during a break, he sought me out. "Want to go to a movie some night.

"Sure."

"How about tonight?"

I hadn't been on a date since I arrived. "Fine."

"I'll pick you up about seven."

"I'll be ready."

It was a warm, clear night. This far north, all the stars seemed to be at my fingertips. After the movie, we drove to a secluded section of beach. We sat in Rusty's car listening to the radio and watching the moon's reflection dancing on the water. A loon's cry echoed across the water as Rusty put his arm around me and pulled me close. "I like a girl who can think. Most girls are feather brains. You have a real head on your shoulders."

"Thanks" I pretended to be flattered. Secretly, I decided that he was conceited. I'd never fall in love with him.

We had fun together anyway. Rusty took me dancing at the country club and sailing at the yacht club. One night we joined a group of sailboats on a moonlight race. The wind blew strong from the south as we pulled away from the yacht club's dock. Other boats surrounded us, but soon we were out in front.

"Hang on," Rusty shouted. "We're going to win."

"I am." Spray soaked my face. We flew along. I could hardly see the water through the darkness. Another boat appeared beside us. I heard a loud 'bang' as it sped past. Suddenly, a hole appeared in the side of our boat. "We're taking water!" I screamed.

"Quick, hold the rudder."

Rusty pulled in the sail until the boat tipped up on her side. He leaned out on the upper side using his weight for balance. He tried to keep the hole above water. I grabbed the tiller and steered for home. "What happened?" I cried through the wind.

"Someone in that boat threw a firecracker. It exploded under us."

We made it to the canoe which was tied to my family's mooring a short distance from shore. Rusty dropped the sail. "Get into the canoe. I'll take care of the boat."

"Okay." I stepped over the side. Just then the sailboat shifted in the wind. I missed the canoe and dropped into the water. Realizing we were in trouble, a group of people had gathered on shore. Rowboats and canoes came out to help us. Hands pulled me into a boat.

Soon I stood shivering on shore. Someone called my name. I turned and there stood Pat. I could hardly believe it!

"Are you all right?"

"Yes. What are you doing here?"

"I drove up from Chicago. I stopped at your house. I met your mother. She liked me, invited me to spend the night."

I grinned, pleased with Mother for a change.

"We heard shouting, so I rushed down here. You sure you're okay?"

I realized I was shaking all over. "I'm freezing."

"I'll take you home. Here. Wear this." He took off his jacket and put it around my shoulders.

"I'm all wet."

"Don't worry water can't hurt it. Come on, you're going home."

"No, I can't. I have to help with the boat."

"Plenty of people are helping with the boat. Look." He waved toward the lake. Canoes and row boats surrounded Rusty. He didn't need me.

"Okay."

We hurried up to the cottage. I took a hot shower while Pat built a fire. We settled down on the couch with steaming mugs of cocoa.

"Feel better?"

"Much. I'm so surprised. I didn't believe you'd really come." I was so happy to see him that I could taste it, but I didn't want him to know that.

"It's not a long drive from Chicago. I wanted to see you. I jumped in the car and here I am."

"I'm glad." I snuggled closer to him.

We were interrupted by loud pounding on the door. Reluctantly, I left Pat and opened it. There stood Rusty. "What are you doing here?" he demanded angrily. "I hunted all over the beach for you."

"I'm sorry, I knew I should have stayed."

"She was wet and cold so I brought her home," Pat explained.

"Who are you?"

"He's a friend of mine from Colorado." I explained. "He just arrived. Pat Haines, meet Rusty Smith."

Pat extending his hand. "I'm happy to meet you."

Rusty, looked angry but he took Pat's hand "Me, too." Then he turned to me, "I'll see you tomorrow at rehearsal."

"Okay." I closed the door after him and turned to Pat.

"Are you going with that guy?"

I shook my head. "Just seeing him casually."

"He didn't sound casual. He acted like he owned you."

"Nobody owns me. It's you I love."

"We need to talk about that."

"All right." I sat back down on the couch. "Is something wrong?"

"Yes. I can't stand the situation the way it is."

"What situation?"

"Loving you. It's driving me crazy. I want you all the time." He stood up and began to pace.

"Is that bad?"

"Yes. I can't stand it. I either have to marry you or break up with you."

"Are you asking me to marry you?"

He answered in a voice so low that I could hardly hear him. "No, I can't. I still have three years of college ahead of me."

"But we love each other."

"It doesn't matter. School comes first."

My heart pounded so loudly that I could hardly think. "What do you suggest?"

"Breaking up. I came to say good-bye."

"Oh Pat." Tears poured from my eyes.

"I'm sorry. I wish I could marry you."

"So do I."

"I'd like to get some sleep now. I have a long drive tomorrow."

"Okay. I'll show you the guest room."

"Thanks."

I pointed out the extra room and then went to bed myself. It took me a long time to fall asleep. I lay in bed crying softly.

Thank goodness guests slept at the other end of the house. Pat couldn't hear me. When I awoke in the morning, he was gone.

"Where's your friend?" Rusty asked at rehearsal.

"Gone. He was just passing through."

"Good."

I dated Rusty the rest of the summer. I felt happy with him, but nothing more. He took me to movies and dances. The play was a smashing success.

In August, Father arrived. He planned to stay a couple of weeks and then drive us all home. It didn't work out that way. We had a long flight of steps in front of the house which led up from our parking area to the door. Father had built a bench on the landing halfway up. "When you start dating, you can entertain your boy friend here," he explained. But when I started to date, he had a spotlight installed above those stairs.

One night, soon after he arrived, I had a date with Rusty.

"I want you home by midnight," Father ordered.

"The dance lasts until one."

"Midnight. Not one minute later."

I nodded, knowing better than to argue with him.

Promptly at midnight, Rusty and I drove up in front of the house. The spotlight burned brightly. I opened the car door and started to get out.

"Stay a minute," Rusty asked. "I want to talk to you."

"Okay." I climbed back into the car

Before he could say anything, the spotlight began to flash on and off.

"What is that?"

"I don't know. I'd better find out."

"Come back down after."

"I'd better not. "

"Then I'll see you tomorrow."

"Good night, Rusty."

I climbed the stairs. At the top, just inside the front door stood Father. He jerked it open and started shouting at me. "I told you midnight. Not five minutes after."

"I was here. Right outside in the car."

"I meant in this house. Not in a car."

I'd never seen him so angry."I wasn't doing anything wrong. Just talking."

"Go to your room."

"Yes, sir."

"Tomorrow you're going home."

Father kept his word.The next day he packed the whole family up. We took the night ferry across Lake Michigan, then drove back to Minnesota. I didn't really care. I wrote to Rusty explaining what had happened.

I needed some surgery to remove an infected cyst. Mother decided this would be a good time to have it done. I went into the hospital. When I awoke from the anesthesia, I saw a vase of long stemmed red roses. "Where did those come from?" I asked my nurse.

"From your father."

"How nice."

Father never mentioned the incident in Michigan and I never understood what I'd done to upset him.

Chapter 6

Colorado without Pat seemed tedious, my classes, carbon copies of high school. In spring, I decided not to return next fall. I applied for admittance to the University of Washington. My dates weren't worth remembering. The only really nice person I met was a friend of Pat's from Chicago named Bruce Kielly. He had come to Colorado to attend the Air Force academy.

Bruce was a slightly built person with shiny dark hair and deep blue eyes. Pat's roommate, Hank introduced us. He called one bright spring day. "Do you want to go to a picnic?"

"With whom?"

"You don't know him, but you'll like him."

"I've heard that before. Okay. I have nothing better to do."

We drove into the mountains on a brilliantly clear spring day. The air smelled of sage and wild flowers. We unpacked Hank's car. His whole fraternity had come up with their friends and dates. Hank brought a girl named Julie whom I had not met.

The men unpacked a charcoal cooker and started roasting venison. I had never tasted deer meat. "What do you think of it?" Bruce asked.

"It's okay. Moist and tender."

"As long as you can forget having seen *Bambie.*"

I Laughed. "Exactly."

"It's sort of like eating a pet, isn't it?"

"Yes. I didn't think you'd understand." I liked him. Most men would have played the big hunter, very macho. He didn't.

"Let's see if Hank brought hot dogs."

He had. I ate them gratefully. After supper Bruce and I took a walk down a winding mountain path. We sat on a bolder to watch a song sparrow building a nest. Her mate sang nearby.

70

We saw butterflies searching for nectar among dry purple flowers and little lizards scooting between pieces of loose rock. Suddenly, the sun dropped behind the mountain. It turned dark fast.

"We'd better get back," I said.

"Yes, in a hurry. We don't want to be left behind."

The trail was hard to follow. There were a lot of loose rocks on it. As we made our way around a particularly difficult turn, Bruce slipped and fell. "Oh," he cried, "I've hurt my ankle."

"Can you walk?"

"Barely."

"I'll help you."

He put his arm around my shoulder. We crept slowly up hill. At last, we reached the parking lot. It was empty! My heart sank. "They've left without us."

"I can't walk out with this ankle."

"What'll we do? It's getting cold."

"I don't know. Let me think." He sat down on a large rock.

I brushed back tears and sat beside him. I was about to panic when a car appeared. Jumping up, I waved frantically. "Help."

" I'm coming," yelled someone from inside the car.

"Oh, Hank," I cried, recognizing the voice, "thank goodness it's you."

The car stopped beside us. "Where have you been? I sent Julie home in another car. I've been driving around looking for you."

"I sprained my ankle," Bruce explained. "We've been limping back up the mountain."

"Get in the car. We're going to be late getting back."

We climbed in gratefully.Squeezed in between Bruce and Hank, I felt exhausted. I fell asleep thinking about Bruce. He's a thoroughly nice person, I decided. If I ever have a son,

I hope he'll be just the same.

Back at the dorm, I was 'roomed' for being late. I never saw Bruce again. School ended and I went home. In September, I transferred to the University of Washington.

The conductor shouted, "all aboard." as I climbed the steps of the west bound Empire builder. I scrambled into my seat just as the train gave a jerk and started to move. This train ran directly from Minneapolis to Seattle. I didn't have to change anywhere. In September of 1949, I was twenty years old and on my way to the University of Washington. I settled into my roomette, hung my coat in the tiny closet and shoved my suitcase under the seat.

After putting my things away. I walked back to the club car located at the end of the train. It offered an excellent view of the countryside. I found a chair and relaxed. The car was almost empty. Two middle aged men in business suits sat sipping drinks. At the end of the car, an older couple were playing bridge with two young men. They laughed a lot like they were having fun.

After a few minutes, one of the young men came over to me. He was nice looking with bleached blond hair and brown eyes set so wide apart that they gave him a surprised look. "Hello." He sat down beside me. "My name's Spike Hunter. Where're you headed?"

"Seattle. I'm going to the University."

"Really? Me, too. I transferred from the University of Michigan."

"I'm a transfer from Colorado."

"How about having dinner with me? We can get to know each other." I didn't know anyone in Washington. I needed friends."Thanks, I'd love it." We spent the evening together and most of the next day. Spike, a junior like me, planned to major in forestry. We sat up late counting tunnels which the train went through. We went through a lot of tunnels before we arrived in Seattle.

"Where are you staying?" he asked as we got off the train." I may call you."

"At the women's dorm. I'll give you the number." ·

"You're lucky, I have to find an apartment."

"Sounds difficult this close to the beginning of class."

"Not really. My fraternity keeps a list of available rooms."

"Good. You'll need it. Well good-bye." We had reached the street. I climbed into a waiting cab and headed for the University.

My dorm was an attractive red brick building with a sunken patio. It housed a lot of women. I felt lucky to have a private room. Most people had roommates.

My tiny corner room had two windows. A radiator stood under one. A closet and the door took up most of the inside wall. There was no place for my bed except along the outside wall. The building was brick with no insulation. My bed felt clammy, cold. I hung a blanket on the wall.It didn't help.I still froze.

I needed permission from each professor before I could take his class.I spent the next few days introducing myself to them. They were all kind to me except for the poetry teacher, professor Rudder. He had a reputation for hating women. "You'll never get into his class," a girl in my dorm told me.

"I might as well try. The worst he can do is turn me down."

"You'll be sorry."

I shrugged and went to see him. I found a huge man with strange eyes like Betty Davis. "What do you want?" he growled as I knocked on his open, office door. He wore a rumpled tweed suit which looked like he'd slept in it. He smelled of stale beer.

I looked him straight in the eye."I want to take your writing class."

"What have you written? Let me see your work." He shook his head for emphasis. "I don't take just anybody."

I had no intention of letting him intimidate me. "I haven't brought anything with me. I'll send for some if you'd like."

My answer surprised him. He sputtered for a moment. "No, that won't be necessary. You can take the class."

"Thank you." I smiled not too politely. "Sign here."

He initialed my card making me one of three women in class.

School went easily. I enjoyed everything except the dorm meals. They were planned by student dietitians and served cafeteria style on army surplus trays. The students' grades were based on feeding us as cheaply as possible. We were given greasy pork and powdered eggs. I ate most meals at a nearby coffee shop. That's where I met Spike again. He walked in as I was eating breakfast. With him was an anemic looking blond who looked too young for college.

"Hi." Spike came up to my booth. "Want company?"

"Sure, sit down."

He waved at his friend. "This is my roommate, Beau Brown."

"Hi, Beau."

"Hi." He and Spike slid into the other side of the booth.

"Beau's a freshman pledge at my fraternity."

"We're not really roommates," Beau explained. "We share the third floor of a private home. We each have our own room."

"We share the bath," Spike added. "It's on the landing halfway up the stairs."

"Odd, but private," Beau added. "We even have our own entrance."

"That's more than I have. Is it far from school?"

"About five blocks. Want to see it?" Spike asked.

"Some other time. I have a class now."

Give me your phone number. I'll call you."

"Sounds good."

Spike called a few days later. "My fraternity is having a dance Saturday. Want to go?"

"Sure, thanks." I was happy for the chance to go out. I still hadn't met many people. My sorority informed me that they didn't accept transfers. I wasn't affiliated with the Seattle chapter so I couldn't be included in their activities.

"We can double date with Beau," Spike continued. "He has a car."

"Sounds good."

On Saturday, Spike arrived alone. "Beau couldn't find a date. We're going with another freshman."

"Okay." I didn't think Beau would be much fun anyway.

His replacement was a pledge named Claude, a freshman who lived in Seattle and drove his mother's car. His date was a pimple faced high school student named Rose.

I nodded as Spike introduced us and climbed into the car. After a few minutes we arrived at a huge warehouse. Inside, someone had hung bunches of balloons from the ceiling. They didn't helped much. The room was still ugly. A band blared at one end. At the other, long tables were decorated with fake flowers. Each table held paper cups and large bottles of soda. The room smelled of bourbon.

Everyone had brought a bottle. Some had several. Spike had bottles of gin and bourbon in a paper sack. "What do you want to drink?"

" 7-Up."

"With gin?" He opened the bottle.

"No. Plain 7-Up."

"Later then." He poured himself a stiff drink.

Up and down the table people were mixing all sorts of strange things. I watched one person mixing scotch with Coca-

Cola. Awful!

"Want to dance?" Spike asked.

"Sure." The band played. A few couples danced. Most of them concentrated on drinking. Spike and I danced for a few minutes. Then Spike wanted more gin.

As time passed, the room became hot and smoky. Towards midnight, my head began to pound. Spike and the others seemed to be drinking as many different kinds of alcohol as possible. Everyone was drunk.

I tugged on Spike's sleeve until I got his attention. "Take me home."

"What?" He looked at me in disbelief. "The party's just started."

"Please It's after twelve. You've already had to much to drink."

I turned to Claude. "Will you take us home?"

"No. not now."

"I'll buy a pizza first."

"I'm not hungry."

"I am," Rose said. "We can come back here after."

"Okay." Claude agreed.

"One last drink." Spike emptied the gin into his cup.

"Bring it with you." I wanted to get started. We piled into the car.

"How about the Pizza parlor near school," I suggested.

"Sounds okay." Claude agreed.

"I don't know," Spike said. "I don't feel so well."

Before we reached the restaurant, Spike turned green. "Stop the car. I'm going to be sick."

Claude couldn't pull over fast enough. Spike threw up.

"My mother will kill me." Claude shrieked. "It's her car."

"Take Spike home," I cried. "Hurry before he's sick again."

We pulled up in front of Spike's house. He staggered out

and stood fumbling with his keys, unable to unlock the door. "I'd better help him." I climbed out of the car. I expected to unlock the door and get back into the car. I never had a chance. Claude gunned the engine and sped away.

"Wait!" I shouted, too late. The car vanished. I stood alone in the dark with a drunken date. What to do? I'd heard that axe murderers hung around college campuses at night waiting to attack young women. Frightened of being alone on the street this late, I opened Spike's door, turned, and ran all the way back to my dorm.

Safe at the door, I tried to calm down and catch my breath. I forced myself to walk calmly through the lobby and up to my room. Once inside, I locked the door and stood with my back against it, crying and shaking. Much later, I showered and dropped into my bed

I never heard from Spike again. Thank goodness. I put the incident out of my mind. I concentrated on my studies. Everything went smoothly except for Professor Rudder's class. His lectures seemed disjointed and hard to follow. He rambled. Then one day he arrived in class looking more disreputable than usual. His clothes were rumpled. His hair stood up all over his head. "I'm not holding class today," he announced looking around nervously. "Where's John? I have to talk to John."

"He's late," someone answered.

"He can't be. John's never late." Rudder started to pace up and down waving his arms. "Hurry up, John." He mumbled something I couldn't understand. He started yelling. He pulled a rolled pair of socks from his pocket and threw it at one of the girls. Tears ran down his face as he screamed, "John, where are you? I need you now."

Seconds later the head of the English department ran into the room. Rudder stopped yelling but sweat poured down his face.

"Class dismissed," the department head said. "Everybody out."

We left quickly. I went home wondering who John was. I found out at the next class. John appeared. Professor Rudder didn't. The head of the English department came in instead. "This class has been canceled," he told us.

"I need it to graduate," someone in the back complained. He was an older student who always came to class dressed in a white shirt, necktie, and the same brown tweed jacket with patches on the elbows.

The professor looked at him. "You're John Thomas aren't you?"

"Yes. I MUST have this class. I'm a graduating senior."

"I'll try to find a teacher for next quarter, but don't count on it."

"Professor Rudder won't be back?"

"Not this year."

After he left everyone stood around. It was too late to substitute another class. "What'll we do ?" someone asked.

"How about having our own class?" someone else suggested.

"Good idea," John agreed. "We can have it at my place."

"Let's go."

They all nodded and started for the door. I hesitated until John stopped and looked at me. "You coming?"

"I guess so."

We walked up a pleasant tree lined street until we came to a residential area about half a mile from school. John lived on the lower level of a split level home. There were windows in front. The back was dug into a hill, so the second story was street level in the back. Even with the windows and a glowing electric wall heater, the room seemed dark and cold. "Take off your coats," John invited. "I'll make coffee."

The coffee tasted terrible. I think he reused old grounds. I learned that John was twenty seven years old. He attended college on the G.I. Bill, a government grant for veterans which provided subsistence living only. John had almost no money.

"Let's all chip in to buy coffee," I suggested putting a quarter on the table. The others nodded.

Although the coffee may have been terrible, the conversation was great. We talked about Walt Whitman and James Joyce. Someone read his own work. I went home feeling like I had made good friends.

My other classes went well. I worked backstage for my theater production class doing costumes for a dance version of Faust. Our teacher had been a professional dancer. He played the lead. At one point he danced up a high tower and then fell off. Two students had to catch him before he hit the floor, very dramatic.

I got to know one of these catchers well because he kept splitting his tights. Every time they tore, he brought them to me for mending. He was a strong, muscular young man named Gentry who looked more like a weight lifter than a dancer. He seemed nice. One night in late fall he asked me out. "My fraternity is having a harvest ball. Would you go with me?"

Memory of the last fraternity dance flashed through my mind. For a moment I froze. I didn't want a repeat of THAT experience. "I'm sorry, Gentry."

I dated John. The school found a substitute teacher. Our writing class was reinstated. After it, our discussion group continued to meet at John's. In addition, I often him went with him to movies or plays.

I liked John. He treated me well and never made any kind of pass. One afternoon during finals week, I developed chills while studying at his house. Teeth chattering, I stood with my back to his electric heater trying to warm up. Soon the smell of scorching wool filled the room. As I Jumped away,the whole back of my skirt fell to the floor in a sooty mass leaving me with my slip showing.

"Now you'll have to marry me," John joked.

"Not today. I've got the flu. I'd better go home."

He walked me to my dorm. "Is there anything I can do?"

"Would you go down to the corner coffee shop and buy me a milk shake? I don't think I'll go to dinner."

"Sure." He looked concerned. "You really shouldn't skip meals. You're studying too hard."

"I guess so."

He brought the shake and read me poetry while I drank it.

"Feeling better now?" he asked when I finished.

"Yes. But I ought to be in bed."

"Okay. I'll see you tomorrow."

"I'm really not going to have much time during finals, John. Maybe we'd better say goodbye until after vacation."

"Are you going home for Christmas?"

"Of course."

"Give me your address. I'll write."

I wrote it out for him. "Bye, John. See you next quarter."

"You can count on it."

Upstairs, I took an aspirin and lay down. I really was sick. I made it through exams, but I still had one problem. How to get back to Minnesota? Eating in coffee shops had been expensive. I had almost no money. Even though Father had given me a round trip train ticket, I had to pay for the roomette myself.They were expensive. I could trade in the first class ticket for a seat in coach. No! What if Father's chauffeur met my train? He'd wonder why I got off the wrong car. Father would ask questions.

I had often heard him screaming at Mother because she overdrew her checking account. I didn't want him yelling at me. I'd better pay for a roomette.

Having made that decision, I gathered up all my books and carried them down to the used bookstore. "Will you buy these?"

"You won't get much for them."

"Whatever it is, I'll take it."

They gave me enough to pay for my roomette. On board the train, in private, I counted my money. I had enough for one meal. If I skipped breakfast, and ate a good lunch, I could do without supper. The next morning, I'd eat a late breakfast at home.

That settled, I relaxed. The gentle movement of the train rocked me to sleep. I had no idea that six months later I would marry John Thomas.

Chapter 7

I arrived home flat broke. Fortunately, the company chauffeur met me at the station. I barely had a nickel for a phone call. At the house, I realized that I had no money for Christmas. Timidly, I went to Mother and asked for a loan. "I only need a few dollars for presents."

"You have to learn to live on your allowance. You can't come begging to me. You know what your father's like. He'd be furious if he found out that I gave you extra money."

"I know. I'm sorry,"

"I'll give you a hundred dollars. You'll have to pay me back. That's the only way I can manage it."

I nodded reliving the nights that I had heard Father yelling at her. It seemed like his angry shouting went on for hours. I shuddered. I didn't want that to happen to me! "I won't do it again. I promise."

I realized that I wanted to get out of that house, away from Father. I needed to be really on my own, out of the Shadow of Gray Tower. I don't know how, I thought, but I'll find a way.

A few days later a package arrived for me. Mother brought it up from the mail box and stood watching while I opened it. "What is it?"

"I have no idea." Unwrapping it, I found a short love poem from John and a little ivory statue carved by Eskimos. How sweet, I thought. John had never mentioned love to me before. He had never even kissed me. I held the statue up for Mother to see. "It's a present." Impulsively, I added, "from the man I'm going to marry." I thought that if I told her I was getting married, it would take her mind off the loan.

"I see. When are you planning to have the wedding?"

"We haven't decided yet. Sometime after graduation."

The more I thought about it, the better I liked the idea.

Why not marry John? He wasn't a threat to me. I had never heard him yell at anyone. Now his Christmas poem told me that he loved me. He was a nice person. I tucked the idea away in my heart.

Next spring, Father wrote to say that he wanted me to go to school in England. I didn't want to go. John was graduating in June. If I went to Europe we'd never be together again, so I asked him to marry me.

John was flabbergasted. "I planned to move into a shack on the beach and write poetry."

"You'd starve."

"What will we live on?"

"I have a little money. Enough to last until you find a job."

"Okay. If you're sure you want to."

We finished exams on Friday and were married on Saturday. I called my parents and invited them to the wedding. They turned me down. "Couldn't you wait a few days?" Mother asked. "We promised to go to an important meeting that weekend."

I had to be out of the dorm by Sunday. We didn't have money for a hotel room. I couldn't tell Mother that "No. We have to be married right away." She'll think I'm pregnant, I knew. I'm not, but I can't help what she assumes.

"You'll have to be married without us."

"I'm sorry," I really didn't care.

"Promise me one thing."

"What?"

"Promise me you'll be married in church."

"All right. I'll ask the Episcopal minister to marry us."

He agreed. We were married in the chapel on a beautiful June day. Four friends from poetry class acted as witnesses. I had no summer clothes with me. I had to wear a blue cocktail dress. I bought a spray of white roses for my hair. John dressed in his one good suit. He looked quite handsome with his shoes shined, hair brushed back and a white carnation in his button hole.

After the ceremony, we went out for pizza. I wanted a nice dinner and a beautiful cake covered with white icing. We couldn't afford it. Pizza cost less. We had no money to spare. After dinner, John and I went to a hotel room for one night. We didn't get much sleep. Our friends had gone out drinking after they dropped us off. They thought it fun to call us on the telephone every couple of hours.

Next morning, we moved into our apartment. "It's impossible." John said a week before the wedding. "We'll never find a place to live near campus."

We were sitting in his apartment reading classified ads. In 1950, the universities were still full of World War Two veterans going to school under the G.I.Bill. Housing was scarce and expensive. We couldn't stay in his apartment, because his roommate wanted to keep it. I didn't like it anyway, too dark and musty.

"Maybe we'll have to look farther away. I can always take the bus to classes next fall."

"Okay, here's one. A cottage for rent at a reduced price to someone who'll take care of the yard."

"Let's go look at it."

"We'd better hurry or someone else will grab it."

We didn't have a car so John's roommate, Charlie, agreed to take us. We drove out to a beautiful country estate with about ten acres of lawns and gardens. The cottage was out away from the main house. "It used to be for guests," the owner explained. "I'll let you have it for $50 a month if you will take care of the yard." She turned to me, "and you can baby sit."

She ought to be paying us, I thought. I didn't argue. "Perhaps."

Outside the cottage, I found an old skinny cat. "Is this

yours?"

"No, it's a stray."

"Poor thing. If we stay here, I'll take care of it."

"No, you won't. My children are allergic to cats. My husband is going to get rid of it"

"Too bad."

The cottage was horrible. It smelled of mildew and a water stain across the living room rug made me think that the roof leaked. The only heat came from a rusty oil stove which had been shoved into a corner of the tiny bedroom. One side of the stove touched the bed, a real fire hazard.

My family would never have asked anyone to live in a place as awful as this, I thought. I never had a chance to say anything to John. The woman never left us alone. John was busy agreeing with everything she said. Before I knew it, he gave her $50 and put the key in his pocket.

Back at the car, I finally had a chance to talk. "I'm not moving in there."

John looked at me in amazement, "What do you mean?"

"It's horrible. I can't live there. Besides, it's miles from a bus line. How will we get to town?"

"I have a bike."

"I don't. I'm not going to be stuck out here."

"Why didn't you say something before I paid her?"

"I never had a chance."

John shook his head. "She'll never give us our money back."

"Then we're out $50."

"It was the cat, wasn't it?" Charlie asked. "You're angry about it."

"No. Not just the cat. Everything was awful."

We found another apartment in a housing project a long way from the University. I would have to take two buses and a ferry to get to classes, but at least it was on a bus line. The rent was only $40 a month. We needed to save money more than ever since we lost $50 on the other place.

The morning after our wedding, Charlie helped John move our clothes. I went shopping for kitchen equipment. I bought dishes, silverware, pans and a few kitchen towels. When I got back to John's apartment he and Charlie were waiting for me. They looked pleased with themselves.

"Look under the couch," John said.

"What?"

"Just do it."

I knelt down and looked. There, in a dark corner, I saw a beautiful little gray kitten. I pulled her out and cradled her in my arms. "What in the world is she doing here?"

"It's your wedding present," John explained. "We passed this sign that said, 'kittens for sale, ten cents.' Charlie stopped. He thought you wanted one."

Charlie nodded. "John picked this one."

"A little girl was selling them to get money for ice cream." John explained. "She only wanted a dime. When I picked out this one, she looked so sad. I thought it must be her favorite. I gave her a quarter."

I was touched. What a thoughtful gift. "She's beautiful, John. Thank you." She really was lovely with long gray hair, a white bib and four little white feet.

"What are you going to call her?"

"Her name's Snook."

Our new home looked like a glorified tenement. We had two rooms at the end of a long ugly building. The bedroom consisted of twin beds, a straight chair and a closet. The living room had a twin bed, a table and four chairs. Between them was a bathroom with a shower and a walk in closet. The kitchen contained a sink, a cupboard, a hot plate and an ice box. A man brought ice twice a week. Food kept more than two days spoiled. Milk soured overnight. All the trash cans for the building were lined up next to our house.

"We've got roaches," John exclaimed the first night.

"How do you know?"

"I turned on the bathroom light and they were everywhere."

"Wonderful," I answered sarcastically.

"Snook thinks so. She's busy chasing them around the shower."

"Do you think she can catch them all?"

John laughed. "I don't think she can catch any."

"What'll we do ?"

"There are cracks in the walls. We could fill them in with something. It might help."

"Let's buy patching plaster."

"And flea powder. Snook's scratching fleas."

"We'll mix flea powder with plaster. That should discourage them."

"Good idea."

It worked. We filled every crack. Soon we were bug free. Roaches weren't our only problem. The neighbors' had a big dog which liked to chase Snook. I thought he might kill her if he ever caught her. I had underestimated Snook. She started sitting in our open window.

One day the dog walked under that window. Snook dropped onto his back plunging all of her claws into his skin. The dog howled in pain. He tried to shake her off. Snook hung on tight. He ran in circles with Snook clinging to his back. Finally the dog freed himself. He ran home with his tail between his legs. He never bothered Snook again.

Every Saturday, John and I took the bus into Seattle to the farmer's market to shop for produce. A dollar bought two sacks of vegetables. For fifty cents, we could sometimes buy a boiled crab. We usually ran out of ice before we could eat all the vegetables. I had to throw some away.

"Why don't we buy less to start with?" I asked John.

"I can't help it. I grew up in Alaska where we had to eat canned vegetables all winter. I go crazy when I see fresh food."

"Makes sense." After that I just tossed out the excess without comment. They hadn't cost that much.

In August, my parents drove out to see us. They came in a new car which they brought as a wedding present for John.

"I'm giving it to him, because he's over twenty five. His insurance rates will be lower than yours." Father explained.

"I see." Although that made sense,I still felt bad . Father had bought cars for both my brothers. It didn't seem fair that I was left out.

"You can still drive it."

"Of course."

Father changed the subject."We've come to take you fishing."

"Fishing?"

"Yes. I've heard that the Olympic peninsula has wonderful fishing."

John nodded enthusiastically. "Steelhead and trout."

"Want to go?"

"You bet."

We drove through a dense rain forest filled with Douglas fir and rhododendrons. It was beautiful, but damp. I found myself shivering even in mid-summer. Eventually, we arrived at a little fishing camp with rustic log cabins and a small store. John and I slept in a huge feather bed. I sank so far into it that I thought I would never get out. Snook thought it was wonderful. I fell asleep with John beside me. When I awoke, he was gone.

"He left with your father at dawn," Mother explained.

"Where did they go?"

"Fishing. Your father hired a guide when he reserved the cabin. They went off with him."

"It'll be kind of dull here for us."

"I brought my needle point."

"I'll take a walk."

After breakfast, I zipped Snook inside my jacket. I headed out into the morning mist. I wandered around looking for birds and wild flowers. I'd never been so cold in summer. Even Michigan seemed warm compared to this. Here the damp cold went right through me. At last, I came to a sunny spot. Taking Snook from my jacket, I sat down on a fallen log to rest.

After a while, I smelled coffee and realized that it had been a long time since breakfast. I hurried back to the cabin. I found everyone drinking huge cups of steaming coffee.

The guide had several large fish broiling on an outdoor grill. Beside them, potatoes sputtered in a heavy skillet. We all stuffed ourselves with food. I don't ordinarily like fish, but these tasted wonderful. When we finished Father sat back and smiled at me. "I have a surprise for you."

"Really. What?"

"John is coming to work for me. I'm planning to buy another company in Wisconsin. John has agreed to manage it for me."

Father had bought a small company in Wisconsin during the 1940s. After World War II, he made Sam president of it.

"Now, I'm going to buy another division. John can manage it after he learns the business."

"What does that mean?"

"He'll start at the bottom and work his way up. My men will train him."

John beamed. "Isn't that wonderful."

"Yes." I didn't dare tell him that it would be harder than it sounded.

My parents took the train home. John and I followed in his new car. After a month's orientation, John was hired as a service representative for Father's new company. We moved into a two bedroom apartment in a private home in Northern Wisconsin. Two nice, gray haired sisters owned the house. They had remodeled the upstairs to make an apartment for the son of one of them. His family had outgrown it. The apartment was nice. It cost $75 a month which included utilities. That was a lot of our $240 monthly income. We ate plenty of cheap tuna fish.

The first morning in our new apartment, I stood at the window watching John drive off to work. It was late September. The leaves had turned bright red and yellow. I smelled wood smoke in the cold morning air. I saw a group of teenagers headed for the bus stop. Suddenly, I felt lonelier than I had ever been in my life. Always before, I had gone to school. Now I had nothing to do. I went downstairs and knocked on the owner's door.

"Come in," a pleasant voice called. "I'm back in the kitchen."

I walked back and found Marie, a plump, gray haired widow with a smile as sweet as apple pie. She took care of the house. Her sister worked in an office somewhere.

"Sit down," Marie invited. "Have a cup of coffee."

"Thanks." I pulled a chair up to the kitchen table. "What can I do for you?" she asked pouring me a cup of strong smelling coffee.

"I wondered if there was a college here. I have a year to finish."

"There's an extension of the University. It only goes through the second year. After that, students have to go to Madison."

"That won't help me. I'm in my fourth year."

"Maybe you could take correspondence courses?"

"Yes, perhaps."

Back in my apartment, I checked with the school. There were no classes which would help me get a degree. Correspondence courses wouldn't cure loneliness, anyway.

"I guess I'll have to get a job," I told John that night at dinner.

"Sounds good to me. What kind of job?"

"I don't know. I'll ask Father."

After dinner, I called home. Mother answered the phone. "I want to talk to Father." I told her. "I need him to help me find a job."

"A job?" Mother repeated hesitantly. "All right, I'll ask him."

A moment later Father was on the phone. "You will not get a job. Do you want people to think the company is in trouble? That it can't pay your husband enough to support you .No.Unthinkable.It would be terrible for business."

"I'm lonely and bored. I have nothing to do."

"Join a church. Go to the women's meetings. It's what your mother does. That's good for business."

"Yes, Father."

"You can come home for your birthday," he said in a softer voice. "It's only a five hour drive. Your birthday falls on Saturday, so John can come, too. I'll take you both to dinner and a show."

"Thank you, Father."

On my birthday, we packed our best clothes and Snook into the car. I felt excited about the play. Father had bought tickets to *South Pacific,* a new musical which everyone said was wonderful. We left early so we'd have time to rest before dressing for dinner.

We took turns driving. I was at the wheel when I suddenly felt dizzy. The car swerved to the right, hit gravel and flew through the air. I felt something whiz past me as we landed. Then everything was still. Slowly, I realized that my eyes were shut. I'm afraid to open them, I thought. What if John is sitting beside me with blood all over him? He might even be dead. I forced myself to open my eyes. I looked at John.

"Are you all right?" He reached over and switched off the ignition.

"Yes. And you?"

"I'm okay. The car isn't. We turned completely over."

"We're right side up now."

"Yes. We were lucky."

"What about Snook? Where is she?"

"I don't know?" He searched the back seat. "She's not here."

"Where could she be?"

"The window beside you is broken. She must have jumped out."

"I felt something fly by me."

"That must have been her."

I was almost crying by now. "We've got to find her."

The car had landed in an empty field far from any houses. Now I heard a siren of an approaching police car. Looking around at the road, I noticed that several cars had stopped.

"I want to go look for her. Quickly, before those people get here."

"Okay. Just don't go far. I'll stay here and talk to the police."

I got out and started to search through tall grass. "Here, Snook."

People who had gotten out of cars started coming towards me. "Have you seen a gray cat?" I asked. They just shook their heads.

John talked to the policeman. Then he called to me. "Come and show this man your driver's license."

"Okay." I came back and handed him the license.

"What happened?" He asked.

"The car skidded. I lost control."

"Yours was the fourth car to miss that curve this year. You're lucky. Somebody's going to be killed on it."

I nodded. "We've lost our cat. Have you seen her?"

"No, sorry."

"I have to look for her."

"You can come back and do that. I've arranged a ride for you to the next town. A bus there will take you into the city. You have to hurry."

"I can't leave my cat."

"Yes, you can," John insisted. "We'll come back for her tomorrow."

"Promise?"

He nodded. "Hurry, come."

We took our suitcase and climbed into a stranger's car. A few minutes later, he dropped us off at a little coffee shop in some tiny town. "The bus stops here," he explained.

John took my arm and started inside. "You're shaking," he exclaimed.

"Yes," I shook so hard that I could hardly talk.

"I'll get you some coffee. I'll call your mother, too."

I nodded. Although the coffee helped, I continued to shake all the way home. I managed to eat dinner. In the middle of *South Pacific*, I started to cry. I couldn't stop. I cried and cried. Everyone in the audience looked at me in dismay. It wasn't that sad a play.

Next day, Father gave us an old car which Don had left behind. You can drive it until the insurance company decides what to do about yours."

"Thanks, Father."

We drove back to where our car stood in the empty field. John looked at it and shook his head. "I think it's a total loss."

"I don't care. Look for Snook."

After an hour of hunting, John found her hiding in a culvert.

"Thank goodness." I ran over. Poor Snook shook all over when I picked her up. "You drive," I told John. "I'll hold her in my lap."

"Okay."

She continued to shake. Snook lived to be sixteen years old. She shook every time she rode in a car. We left her home whenever possible.

I never understood exactly what had happened that day on the highway. I think I had a dizzy spell. I didn't know that pregnant women sometimes have dizzy spells. A month later, I asked a doctor about it.

"Quite possible," he answered.

"If I'm pregnant, why didn't I lose the baby during the accident? We hit awfully hard."

"I don't know. Some women can step off a curb and miscarry. Others can go through all kind of things without losing the baby."

"So I'm really pregnant?"

"You are. Definitely."

I fixed a nice dinner that night. After we'd eaten I told John. "The baby's due the first week in July."

"Wonderful. Now you won't be lonely any more."

Chapter 8

I awoke screaming. I found myself sitting bolt upright in bed, shivering. My body wet with sweat.

"What's wrong?" John asked from beside me. "That nightmare?"

"Yes." I had dreamt about a ballroom with dark red velvet curtains in a huge, empty house. When I found myself there, I panicked and ran from empty room to empty room searching for a way out. I had experienced the dream before. Something about my pregnancy brought it back. "I'm all right, now," I told him. "Go back to sleep."

"Are you sure?"

"Yes, I'm fine." I was except for the nightmares. They'll pass in time, I told myself. Otherwise, the pregnancy progressed normally. Towards the end of it, Father decided we should buy a house. "I'm promoting John to assistant office manager," he told me over the telephone. "It means more money. You can afford a house."

"That's wonderful. We'll start looking right away."

On Saturday, we started house hunting. It didn't take long to find one in a nice older neighborhood near the high school. The streets were lined with lovely old elm trees and the large four bedroom houses were filled with children.

"It's perfect," I told Father over the phone.

"Good. I'll drive up on the weekend to look at it."

He arrived the next Saturday and we took him to see it. He shook his head. "No. This one won't do," he told the agent. "The stairs are too steep and dark. They need something with a nice open staircase."

"What about the neighborhood? Do you like it?"

Father nodded. "The houses and yards are well kept ."

The agent nodded. "Most people here are professionals.

Doctors, teachers and company managers."

"Have you other houses for sale in this area?"

"There's a nice corner house in the next block, but it's been neglected and needs work."

"Show us that one."

"Certainly." He took us around the block to a white frame house with a porch on two sides. An old wooden swing hung from the porch roof and a large apple tree dominated the back yard.

"This house belongs to an elderly couple who have been renting out the bedrooms. It needs a lot of cleaning."

Father walked through it nodding approval. The rooms were large and well lit. The staircase broad and open. "All it needs is a good scrubbing and a new kitchen." He turned to John. "I have a display kitchen at my office which came out of a trailer. I'll give it to you. All you have to do is clean and paint. Can you do that?"

"Sure."

"Then it's settled." He turned to the agent. "They'll take this one."

"What about financing?"

"I'll arrange that."

The house needed a more work than Father had estimated. We needed a plumber to install the kitchen sink and mend a leak in the sewer. A plasterer repaired walls where old cabinets had been. An electrician rewired the entire house. On the fourth of July, John finished painting.

We moved our furniture in on the fifth. That night I had a little bleeding. I called Mother over the phone.

"That means you'll start labor within twenty four hours," she explained. Your Father and I are all packed. We'll drive over tomorrow."

"You don't have to. We can handle it."

"We're coming."

"If you want to." I really didn't think either of them would be any help. They had bought most of the baby's things so I was grateful.

By afternoon, my labor had really progressed. "I think we'd better head for the hospital," I told John.

"What about your parents?"

"I'll leave them a note. They'll find us."

"Okay."

Lightening flashed in the western sky as John drove me to the hospital.I was too excited to care.At the hospital, a nurse examined me. "Will this be your first delivery?"

"Yes."

"You're in for a long wait. First babies take about seventeen hours." She showed me to a room and left. John came in and sat around yawning. Eventually, Mother and Father showed up. Father looked especially uncomfortable. He paced for a few minutes, then turned to John. "Give me the key to your house. I have a few phone calls I want to make."

"Okay. There's nothing you can do here."

Hours passed. Outside the wind howled and rain poured down. Inside, my labor grew increasingly painful.Finally, a nurse came in and gave me an injection of something. She wheeled me into a special labor room.

I felt afraid. "I want my husband with me."

"No. Your husband must stay outside. No one is allowed in the labor room but patients."

She put me in a bed and left me. The room was almost dark. I could hear someone in the next bed. A scream filled the air. The nurse came running in. She checked the other woman, then wheeled her away.

I don't know how long I lay alone in the dark. Pains came and went. Eventually, a nurse appeared carrying a flashlight.

She lifted the sheet and checked me. "My God! I can see the hair on its head."

She hurried out of the room. Returning,she wheeled me into the bright light. As my eyes adjusted, I saw that it was the delivery room. Someone moved me onto an uncomfortable table. Someone else forced my legs into cold metal stirrups.

My doctor walked in. Thank goodness!. He nodded at me, then spoke to someone standing behind my head. "Okay. Make her comfortable."

The person put a mask over my face. I didn't mind until the contraction began. Then I felt like I was smothering. I shook my head frantically from side to side until I dislodged the mask. I gulped in huge quantities of air.

"You can breathe with the mask on," a voice said. "There's air in it."

"Not enough." I didn't have time to argue, another contraction had begun.The mask went back over my face. As soon as the contraction eased I shook it off. This time the anesthesiologist let me. I gulped air until the start of the next contraction when he covered my face again.

At the same time, my doctor yelled, "push, push."

I obeyed pushing hard until something popped out. Then I relaxed.

"No, no," he cried. "That's only the head. Keep pushing."

I took a deep breath and bore down hard. Something inside me came spiraling out. It felt like a ball of string unraveling.

The doctor bend down and lifted up my baby. He held it up high so I could see. "It's a boy."

I only had a quick peek before a nurse took it away. The doctor turned his attention back to me. "I had to cut you," he explained. "If I hadn't you would have been badly torn. I'm going to sew you up now."

I nodded. This time I didn't fight the mask.

When he finished, someone wheeled me out through a dimly lit hall into my even darker room. John and Mother were waiting. "The power's out," John explained . "We've had a bad storm."

"The phones are dead, too," Mother added .

John explained. "They wanted me to go fetch your doctor. Just as I was leaving, he walked in the door."

"Thank goodness. He barely arrived in time."

"I know. He tried to call the hospital. His phone was dead, so he jumped in his car and came."

I nodded. "Good. I'm tired now. I want to sleep."

"We'll leave," Mother said. "It's very late."

"Good night. Sleep well."

"I will."

A few minutes later a nurse arrived with my baby. "You didn't have a chance to look at him in the delivery room." She held a flashlight on him. "See. He's perfect."

"Can I hold him?"

"Of course."

She put him down beside me. I held him close and felt a kind of love I had never known before. It was as though all my warm feelings were focused on this one little boy. I could love him without reservation. It was a new experience for me. I kissed him gently on his head.

"You must rest now," The nurse said reaching down to pick up the baby. "He'll be in the nursery. We'll bring him to you in the morning."

"Okay."

A baby! How wonderful! I lay there in the dark too excited to sleep. I heard footsteps and whispering in the hall. It's time to feed the baby, I thought coming fully awake. It wasn't the baby, It was Father.

"Are you still here?" he asked.

What a funny thing to say, I thought. Where else would I be? But I didn't say that. "Hello, Father. Did you see the baby?"

"No. Have you had it?"

"Yes. A boy."

"Good. I like boys."

"His name's Bruce." I said remembering the promise I had made to myself in Colorado.

"When did you decide to name him that?"

"A long time ago."

"I see."

"You can look at him if you want. He's in the nursery."

"I'll take a look on my way out."

"Good night, then."

"Night." He disappeared into the darkness.

In the morning, I learned that Father had flown out at dawn to attend an urgent meeting in New York. He mailed back a postcard with a picture of an airplane addressed to 'Bruce Collins.' It said, "Welcome, young man. May your journey be a pleasant one." The card surprised me. Father had made the side trip to see us instead of taking a train to his business meeting. He must care about us, I realized. Father hated to fly.

Summer faded into fall, then winter. Before I knew it Bruce was two years old. I loved being a mother. Holding Bruce gave me a feeling which I had never known before. My life had new purpose and direction. I met other mothers as I wheeled his carriage around our block.

The neighborhood was filled with children. Across the street lived a tall, dark haired child named Timmy Baak who was almost the same age as Bruce. I liked his mother immediately. Lois, was both beautiful and friendly. She was tall and slender with dark hair which she wore up in a bun. She had a wonderful laugh. Timmy and Bruce became great friends.

I met Connie Jepsen, a short stocky blond who lived down the block. Connie had six children. Bruce never lacked playmates.

One bright July morning, I invited these two mothers and their children over to help celebrate Bruce's second birthday. I had planned games for the children. They never played them. The big attraction was kittens. Snook had four kittens, three little black fluff balls with white feet and one solid gray long haired beauty. Even though the kittens could run faster than children, chasing them kept everybody busy until lunch .

The children sat around my dining room table.They tried to look grown up. I gave them colored hat and a paper whistle with feathers in the end. Soon they were jumping around, screaming and tickling each other.

"That's enough," Lois cried. "You're much too wild."

"I'll get the cake." I brought in a chocolate cake with two candles. "Okay now, blow out the candles." I told Bruce.

He took a deep breath, held it for a moment and then smashed his fist into the top of the cake. I snatched it out of his reach. "I guess he's too young for blowing out candles."

Lois looked at Connie."You'd never guess this was her first child."

"Never,"

I served the children slices from the undamaged side of the cake. The rest of the day went smoothly. I had the mess cleaned up and dinner ready by the time John arrived work. "How did the party go?" He asked as he sat down to eat.

"Fine. the kittens were a big hit."

"And the food?"

"It was okay."

John laughed. "Aren't going to tell me what happened to the cake?"

"You saw it?"

" I looked in the refrigerator."

Just then the phone rang. I jumped up. "I'll answer it."

"Happy Birthday to Bruce," a voice said on the phone.

"Hi, Father. He's asleep."

"That's okay. Just wish him a Happy Birthday from me."

"I certainly will."

"Let me speak to my new assistant manager. The board promoted your husband today. I called to tell him about it."

"That's wonderful. I'll put him on."

"When we finish your mother wants to talk to you."

"All right. Hang on a minute."

I called to John. "It's Father."

I watched as John took the phone. His face lit up with a big smile. "That's wonderful. Thank you. I hope I do a good job."

He handed the phone back to me. "Your mother wants to speak to you."

I nodded. "Hello, Mother."

"My mother will be seventy five in August and she wants to have a family reunion in Michigan. I expect you to come."

"What about John?"

"It'll be over the Labor Day weekend. John won't miss work."

"We'll have to bring Bruce, too."

"That's fine."

"Okay. We'll see you then."

John had returned to the dinner table. He was still excited. "Guess what? I got a raise."

"I know. Father told me. Now we can have another baby."

"I thought we'd buy a new car."

"Let's do both."

Summer passed quickly Before I knew it the Labor Day weekend arrived. We didn't have a new car, but I thought I was pregnant. It was too soon to be sure so I didn't tell anyone.

I felt squeamish as I packed for our trip. It would be a long hot drive in the back seat of my parents car to Manitowoc. We would take a ferry across Lake Michigan. Then another hot drive across Michigan to the party at my aunt's home in Detroit. I didn't want to go, but I didn't want to explain my reluctance either.

By the time we arrived in Detroit the temperature had reached one hundred degrees. I had a splitting headache. Bruce had not handled the crossing well. All he wanted to do was scream.

"Can't you do something for him?" John asked me at the motel.

"He's hot. Maybe a cool bath will help."

"I'll take him in the shower with me."

"Good. I'll lay down. I feel as bad as he does."

"Don't you start crying, too. I couldn't handle that."

"Don't worry. I'll lie quietly with a cold cloth on my head."

John nodded as he peeled off his clothes.

Bruce quieted down after his shower. Eventually we all slept.

Much to my relief, the new day was cooler. After breakfast we drove out to my aunt's home. Her husband was a successful architect. They lived in a lovely country place with a rolling lawn and mature shade trees.

Relatives roamed everywhere. Mother recognized most of them. They were all strangers to me except Granny. She sat in a comfortable rocker under a lovely old oak. She was still a handsome woman with gray hair curled tightly against her head. She looked especially nice in a cool blue linen dress. I liked her even though, I hadn't spent much time with her.

As I went to greet her, I passed a tent which had been set up in the yard. I saw tables with cold drinks and a mountain of food. I took one look at the fried chicken and made a dash for the house. Morning sickness, I thought as I came out of the bathroom.

"Hi Granny," I said coming up to her. "How do you like your party?"

"I love it, except for the heat. I should have been born in spring."

"You didn't have much choice in that." I handed her a package. "Here, I've brought you a gift."

"You didn't have to do that." She fumbled with the wrappings.

"It's a picture of Bruce. I thought you'd like it."

"It's lovely. He looks like you."

"I thought he looked like his father."

Granny smiled. "Maybe just a little."

At that point another grandchild interrupted us. I went off to find John and Bruce. My headache had returned. I felt really nauseous. I was thankful when Father decided it was time to leave.

At the motel I lay down with another cold cloth on my head. Bruce napped beside me while John played cribbage with Father.

"Since it's the end of the Labor Day weekend, the boat will be crowded tomorrow," he told John. "I'll try to get a cabin even though it's a daylight crossing. That way Bruce will be able to take his nap."

"Good idea."

Father was right. At the dock, we found cars lined up for a block waiting to board. Father got out of the car. "The rest of you stay here. I'll go arrange for the cabin."

John nodded and slipped behind the wheel.

We inched forward as one car after another was loaded on to the boat. Finally, Father returned waving tickets. "It's all arranged. We can board."

He climbed in and pulled our car out of line. He drove

ahead until we reached the ship. A member of the crew drove our car on board. I felt guilty seeing all those people waiting in line behind us. I couldn't worry about that. I had started to bleed. I needed to get on board where I could relax.

On deck, I sat in a chair next to Mother. "Look at all those people getting on. At this rate there won't be enough chairs to go around."

"Father was right to book a cabin,"

Mother looked around searching for him. "Where is he?"

"John and Bruce are walking around the deck. Maybe he's with them."

"Yes, probably. Oh, look. There're Dr. and Mrs. Grosse."

She stood up and waved at them. "Come on over here."

Mrs. Grosse walking over. "The ship is really crowded , isn't it?"

"Yes." Mother turned to me. "Get up and give Mrs. Grosse your chair."

"I'll go get some more chairs." I couldn't find a single empty chair. "I think I'll find Bruce and put him down for his nap," I told Mother. "I'm tired so he must be, too."

"All right, dear," she answered indifferently.

I didn't have any trouble finding John and Bruce. They were back at the stern watching our crew load automobiles into the cavernous hold. Ordinarily, it carried forty railroad cars across Lake Michigan along with a few automobiles and passengers.

Today, so many people wanted to cross that the freights had to wait. The hold was rapidly filling with automobiles. Bruce stood on the rail watching while John held him so he couldn't fall.

"Hi darling," I said to Bruce. "Are you tired? How about a nap?"

"I'm not sleepy."

"Yes, he is," John disagreed. "Take him inside."

"Come on, Bruce." I took his hand and led him into the saloon.

I had been on these ships often enough to know which cabin Father would buy, the corner one. It had two bunks, a port hole and a fan.

The door was closed, so I knocked. "Come in," Father's voice answered. Inside, Father lay stretched out on one of the bunks. The room felt incredibly stuffy. The little fan simply pushed hot air around.

"Whew!" I said. "How can you stand it in here?"

"There weren't any chairs left on deck so I came in. It'll be cooler as soon as we get out on the lake. Are we loaded yet?"

"Just about. I brought Bruce in for a nap."

Father nodded. The whistle sounded almost drowning out his next words. "That's it. We're casting off."

"Good." I lifted Bruce into the other bunk and climbed in beside him. I felt sick and exhausted. I was bleeding hard. Thank goodness that Dr. Grosse is on board, I thought. I might need him. I'm afraid I'm having a miscarriage.

Chapter 9

I opened my eyes in a room filled with sunshine. Someone had opened the curtains. The sudden burst of light hurt my eyes. I closed them again and lay thinking. How long had it been? The last day I remembered clearly, I was aboard ship. It had been summer and hot.

Now as I opened my eyes cautiously and looked outside, I saw bare tree limbs. Where had the leaves gone? Where had autumn gone? I had no idea. My memory was a blur. I knew that I was in a hospital. I had no idea how long I had been ill. Could it really be winter now?

I tried to sit up to get a better look outside. I couldn't move. My right arm was taped to a board. Something in a bottle dripped down through plastic tubing into my hand. It hurt and so did my stomach. Using the other hand, I reached down to touch my stomach. All I could feel was tape. My entire abdomen was encased in a girdle of tape! I panicked! What had they done to me?

I must have cried out, because in a moment a nurse appeared. "You're awake. Good. I'll tell the doctor."

"What happened to me?"

"Your doctor will explain. He'll be here in a moment."

She disappeared leaving me with no choice but to wait. I must have drifted off to sleep again. The next thing I knew a doctor who looked only vaguely familiar stood bending over me. "How do you feel?"

"Terrible. What happened to me?"

"You had an ectopic pregnancy. That's a pregnancy which lodges in the fallopian tube instead of the uterus. The tube ruptured. You should've come to a doctor sooner."

"I thought I'd had a miscarriage and that I'd recover."

"Wrong. You had a belly full of blood. I had to remove the

107

tube and mop out all that blood. It was a mess. We almost lost you, but you're okay now."

"Thanks. Can I get up ?"

"Maybe later. After we get some food in you. You'll be weak."

He was right. I couldn't even sit up without help. If a nurse helped me up I could walk around, but just barely. I ate everything they brought me in an effort to regain my strength.

After a week, my doctor peeled the tape off my stomach. He checked the stitches. "Good. They're ready to come out. Then you can go home."

"Wonderful," I lied. I felt terrified. I was afraid that if he took the stitches out, I would come apart, unravel somehow. I didn't want to see the incision either. I forced myself to look. I saw a huge red scar which stretched down from my navel. The doctor worked busily cutting and pulling out stitches. "Everything looks fine. You can go home tomorrow."

"That's great," I answered both excited and scared. After he left, I called John. He promised to come first thing in the morning to pick me up. Nervous, I slept poorly. Next morning, I dressed after breakfast. The exertion exhausted me. I climbed back into bed and lay there fully clothed waiting for him.

"Are you all right?" he asked when he saw me.

"I'm a little weak."

"You look like hell. Still, it'll be nice to have you home. You had me worried."

"I'm sorry. Is Bruce all right?"

"He's worried about you. He missed you."

"I missed him, too."

"I've a woman to look after you both. All you have to do is get well."

"Sounds good to me. Can she cook?"

"She's not the greatest, but I managed to eat it."

The drive home was uneventful. I spent it looking out the window. I wondered how winter could have come so fast. It had been summer. I had been aboard ship and bleeding. Now I remembered. I made it home okay. I seemed to be better, so I hadn't mentioned it to anyone.

I would have felt foolish going to my doctor. How could I tell him I thought I was pregnant while doing all that bleeding? I just kept quiet. My stomach hurt for a long time. I thought I would get over it. I didn't.

Finally, I went to my doctor. He listened to my story and then said, "I want a specialist to see you in the hospital. I want you to go in today."

In the hospital a strange doctor poked my stomach until I cried out in pain. "Does that hurt?"

I nodded.

"I'm a surgeon. I want to put you to sleep and have a little look in there. It's just an exploratory. I don't think I'll find anything serious."

"Okay," I agreed. That's all I remembered. Now it was winter. I was on my way home with rubbery legs and a huge scar down my stomach.

When we reached the house, I saw Bruce waiting at the window. He rushed to meet me. "Mommy you're home," he cried as I opened the door.

"Hello, darling." I gave him a big hug. "I'm glad to see you."

"I'm glad, too. Are you dead?"

"No, honey, I'm not dead. Where did you hear that word?"

"The lady who took care of me said it. What's 'dead' mean, Mommy?"

"Never mind. I'm fine. I'm going to get well and take care of you. But right now I have to go upstairs and lie down. Want to come?"

"Yes. I made you a present."

"Show me." I took his hand and started upstairs. John followed carrying my suitcase.

"It's in your room." Bruce pulled me upstairs and into the bedroom. "Here." He pointed to the wall next to my bed. On it I saw a large face drawn with lipstick. "It's to keep bad dreams away."

"Have you been having bad dreams?"

He nodded.

"You won't be have them anymore." I sat down and held him close. "Everything is all right now."

I kept that face on my bedroom wall. It must have worked. Bruce stop having nightmares. Eventually, John repainted the room. Until then, that bright red face remained as our protector.

My recovery was slow. I still felt weak as Christmas approached. I decided to buy my gifts from mail order catalogs. For Bruce, I ordered a set of giant blocks and an imitation store with miniature groceries. They came in a large carton which I put away until Christmas eve.

"These can be his gifts from Santa Claus," I explained to John. "We'll unpack the box after he's asleep and put them under our tree."

"Good idea. That way neither of us has to trudge around town hunting for presents."

On Christmas eve, Bruce helped John and I decorate our tree. Then I took him upstairs and tucked him into bed. John got out the box of toys. As soon as Bruce fell asleep, I hurried down to see how everything looked.

I expected to find presents beautifully arranged. Instead, I saw John sitting on the floor surrounded by huge pile of cardboard. I could hear him swearing under his breath. He looked up as I came in. "Didn't the catalog explain that these toys came unassembled?"

I stared at him. "I don't know. Maybe. It never occurred to me."

"I'm going to be up all night. There are a thousand pieces here."

"I'll help." I sat down beside him and picked through the pile of cardboard. There were big pieces which formed the sides of the store and small ones which had to be folded and glued into miniature cereal boxes or loaves of bread. Even the blocks had to be assembled and glued.

"I'll take the little ones." I picked up a piece which said 'corn flakes.'

It didn't take us the whole night. About 2:30 AM I glued the last little box together as John placed the store front next to our tree. I turned the colored lights on and stood back to admire the scene. "It looks great. Thanks, John."

"My pleasure. But next year lets buy stuff that's put together."

"It's a deal."

"Can we sleep now?"

"In a minute. We have to eat cookies first."

"What cookies?"

"The ones Bruce left for Santa Claus." I pointed to a plate which Bruce had left on the mantle. "Here, have one."

"Thanks. I am hungry at that."

"Make sure you leave a few crumbs on the plate."

"Okay." He gulped down the cookies and headed upstairs. "I'll bet I'm in bed before you are."

"I'm right behind you. I just have to turn out the lights."

Upstairs, I fell asleep so quickly that I have no memory of my body hitting the bed. It seemed only a matter of seconds before the bedroom door crashed open. "Mommy, mommy Santa's been here. I found presents downstairs and the cookies are all gone."

I opened one eye and saw Bruce standing in the doorway holding the empty plate. John rolled over and groaned. "What time is it?"

"It's morning. Time to get up," Bruce answered.

I squinted at the clock. "It's six-thirty."

"That's the middle of the night."

"Not to a child."

John rolled out of bed. "Okay. I'm up."

Christmas was nice despite our lack of sleep. The presents were a big success. Bruce played with that store for years and the huge blocks proved to be almost indestructible.

Two years passed quickly. John bought Bruce a fishing pole for his fourth birthday. "You're old enough now," he explained.

"Oh boy! When can we go?"

"Soon."

He kept his word. In August, he told Bruce to get out his rod because, "next Saturday, you're going fishing."

"Can I go, too?" I asked. "Or is this trip just for men?"

"She can come, can't she Dad?"

"Of course. We'll stay overnight at a lodge."

On Saturday, we drove up into northern Wisconsin. The sun shown brightly as we set out. It dimmed as we drove into a deep, silent forest. Here the air hung heavy with the scent of pine. We rounded a curve and saw a big buck deer standing at the edge of the road. He stood looking at us, curious, but unafraid. John stopped the car so we could watch him.

"What a magnificent animal."

"Why doesn't he run away?" Bruce asked.

"He probably has a family nearby. Look carefully. You might see a mother deer or a fawn."

We sat quietly watching. Before long, something moved in the high brush. A doe burst out, running. Beside her was a tiny spotted fawn. In a second they disappeared. The buck reared up on his hind legs, snorted once and followed them.

John restarted the car. In few minutes we saw our lodge. It was a large, solitary building with a neatly mowed lawn stretching down to the bank of beautiful lake. A path led to a small dock where several boats were tied. Inside, we found a large room with worn leather furniture arranged around a stone fireplace. Pine logs burned cheerfully giving the room a warm, friendly glow. Even though it was summer, the heat felt good.

"Welcome" the owner said as he came to greet us. He was a stocky man with graying hair. He had big, strong hands which made me think of a lumber jack. "You must be hungry after your long drive. My wife has dinner ready." He pointed to the dining room where several people sat eating.

I could smell the aroma of freshly baked bread. "I'm starved."

"Me, too," Bruce added.

Our host nodded and took the suitcase from John. "I'll take this up to your room. You can go in to dinner."

The dining room was quite remarkable. A high shelf ran around all four walls and on it was an incongruous assortment of things. Near our table, I saw a statue of a girl in a flowing white dress, a toy bear and an assortment of vases. I asked our waitress where they came from.

"This lodge is closed during winter. The owners travel. They bring back souvenirs. They've been doing it for thirty years. They have all this stuff. Amazing, isn't it."

"Yes."

Dinner tasted wonderful. I usually hate fish, but this was delicious. They served fresh trout from the lake which had been boned and then baked in a beer batter. With it, we had home grown tomatoes and warm cloverleaf rolls. For dessert, we were served hot apple pie topped with ice cream. As we ate, a little bird flew over our heads. It disappeared into one of the nearby vases.

"What was that?" John asked.

"It's a parakeet," the waitress answered. "She's nesting in that vase. She keeps laying eggs. Of course, they never hatch."

"Poor thing." I felt sorry for the bird. John had a different perspective. He waited until the waitress left. Then he said, "I'll bet the health department would have a fit if they knew there was a bird flying around in the dining room."

I laughed. "Yes. This place is so far out in the woods that the health department probably never comes here."

John nodded. "And who cares. The food is wonderful."

After dinner the owner showed us to our room. Our bed was a large four poster with a feather mattress which was so soft that I didn't think I would ever be able to get out of it. Next to it, Bruce's little bed looked like a Roman couch. He slept well.

We awoke to the smell of coffee. Downstairs our hostess greeted us. She was a rosy cheeked woman with gray hair pulled back in a bun. "Welcome." She showed us to a table by the window. "We have pancakes for breakfast. Do you want them with strawberries and whipped cream?"

"Do you have syrup?" Bruce asked.

"Of course."

"I'd like the strawberries," John said.

"I'll bring both."

She served us a huge platter of pancakes, a pitcher of melted butter and steaming mugs of strong coffee. "I'll come back with milk for the boy."

I stared at the platter. "It's too much food. We can't eat all that."

"If you're going to fish, you need food. Fishing makes people hungry."

"Don't worry, I can handle it," John declared.

"Me, too," Bruce added.

After breakfast, we rented a boat. Fog hung low over the water as John started the motor. We headed out onto the lake and around a point towards a spot where the owner told us we would be sure to catch fish.

"You'll see some dead trees near shore," he explained. "Fish lie in among them. All you have to do is cast nearby."

We found the place and dropped anchor just as the fog lifted. John opened his tackle box and took out a lure. He found a can of insect repellent, too. "Here, put some of this on." He offered it to me. "The flies are bound to get bad as soon as the sun comes out."

"Okay." I took the can from him and sprayed some on my arms.

Our host certainly knew his lake. We hardly put our hooks in the water before fish took the bait. Even Bruce caught several little blue gills. After a while he grew tired of fishing.

"Put us ashore," I told John. "I'll take him for a walk."

"Okay, but stay nearby. There could be bears in these woods."

Bruce and I walked along the shore gathering pretty stones and frightening an occasional crayfish. As we turned a corner, I saw an amazing sight, a pile of tiny butterflies. They looked as though some giant had poured them out of a bucket onto the beach. I had never seen anything like it. "What are they doing?"Bruce asked.

"I have no idea."

Back at the boat, I told John about them. "Have you ever seen a pile of butterflies like that?"

He shook his head. "And I probably never will. It's time we headed back. I'm hungry."

"Me, too," Bruce agreed.

We took the larger fish back to our host. "I'll clean them and pack them in ice for you to take them home. Pick them up after lunch."

"They'll make nice gifts for the people at work," I told John.

"You mean you're not going to cook them ?" John looked hurt.

I shook my head. "Not a chance."

Back home, as I was taking my bath, I noticed a fine rash developing on my arms. I showed it to John. "You must be allergic to something."

I nodded. "Probably fish."

On Monday, I awoke to discover that I could not bend my elbows. My fingers were the size of sausages. A red rash covered both arms spreading up my neck to my face. John took one look at me and gasped. "I think I'd better call your doctor."

"Yes."

The doctor agreed to see me so I asked my neighbor, Connie, if she would keep an eye on Bruce.

"Of course I'll watch him." Connie answered, but she stared at me in disbelief. "You look awful."

"I know."

"It's all set," I told John when I returned.

"Good. I'll drop you off on my way to work."

At his office my doctor looked me over carefully. "Were you exposed to anything unusual, a strange plant or some kind of chemical?"

"I had insect repellent on my arms."

"That's probably the cause. I don't think it's serious. I'll give you some lotion which should clear it up."

"Good." I felt relieved. "But there is something else. I think I'm pregnant."

"Okay. I'll run a test. You want another baby don't you?"

"Yes." I grinned at him.

"I'll call you with the results."

That night, I covered myself with lotion. It didn't help much. At least it hid the spots. Slowly, the rash faded. My arms returned to normal size. Finally, the doctor called with the results of my pregnancy test. "Congratulations. You're going to have another baby."

March came in like a lion. By mid-month, soft, fresh drifts of snow lay deep in our driveway. "I'd better keep it plowed," John decided. "We might need the car one these nights."

I nodded. I hadn't said anything to John or my doctor, but I was worried about this baby. It didn't feel right. I kept hoping it would correct itself. That never happened. I went into labor feeling upset.

"Where are the pains?" a nurse asked when I told her.

"They start in my back and come around to the front."

"That's okay."

"It's not. There's something wrong."

She shook her head. "You're nervous because you lost your last baby. This will fix you up." She picked up a needle and stuck it in my arm.

The drug made me groggy and slowed down labor. It didn't stop me from worrying. By the time I reached the delivery room, I was frantic. Even though I pushed and pushed, nothing happened. My doctor stood nearby talking to the nurse. He sounded angry. "Why didn't you call me sooner?"

"I'm sorry, doctor."

"You should have recognized this."

I didn't hear any more. I had another contraction. When it passed, I glanced up. I saw the obstetrician who had operated on me during my last pregnancy. His presence verified all my fears. I took one look at him and burst out crying.

"Stop that," the nurse commanded. I couldn't stop. I just cried harder. "Stop that," she said again. Then she slapped me.

I gasped and stopped.

"Okay, put her out," my doctor said.

It was the last thing I heard. I awoke in my room. As I opened my eyes, I saw John sitting nearby. He smiled at me."You're all right."

"And the baby?"

"She's fine, too."

"Thank God!" I burst into tears again. This time they were tears of relief. Finally, I managed to stop. "She? It's a girl?"

"Yes. A beautiful girl."

"Her name's Jenny." I felt as though I had to name her immediately, to give her an identity so that I couldn't lose her.

"Jenny's fine with me."

Later the obstetrician came in to explain what had happened. "You had a posterior delivery. The baby was facing in the direction way. I had to go in and turn her."

I nodded.

"I wanted to explain before you saw her. She has some marks on her face. Don't worry. They'll disappear."

"All right," I answered. I trusted him.

"How do you feel?"

"Terrible. I really hurt down there."

"Naturally. You can't get hit by a truck and not feel it." He shook his head. "Never mind. I'll give you something for pain."

"Can I see my baby?"

"I'll have her brought in."

A few minutes later a nurse arrived with Jenny. I held her close and saw her little, scratched face. I kissed her gently on the forehead. "I'm sorry, Jenny. You've had a pretty hard start."

Soon two nurses came in. One of them was carrying a hypodermic needle. "We have to take the baby now," she said showing me the needle. The doctor wants you to have this."

"Okay." I handed Jenny to the other nurse. "Take good care of her."

"We will."

The first nurse stuck me with the needle. I fell asleep almost instantly. I awoke to find a nurse standing beside the bed holding my baby. "Good morning." She smiled. "Here's a hungry girl for you to feed."

I reached up and took her into my arms. "Hello, Jenny," I whispered after the nurse had left. "What a funny looking little thing you are."

She did look strange with those marks on her face. They didn't matter. Her scratches would disappear and so would my pain. Jenny was worth it!

She brought an incredible amount of love with her, a new kind of love. I had formed strong ties with Bruce. This bond with Jenny seemed even stronger. She was a girl, like me. An extension of myself. All the good in me had been reborn in Jenny.

She didn't look like me. She had her father's dark curly hair and fair skin. Gently, I touched her little cheek with my finger. "Your skin's so pale that it's almost opaque, like a fragile doll. You need special care. I won't let you grow up in the shadow of a scary house like Gray Tower."

Jenny gurgled agreement and started to nurse. I felt more relaxed with her than I had with Bruce. We settled into an easy routine. By the time we were ready to go home, Jenny's marks had almost disappeared.

Mother had come to stay with Bruce while I was in the hospital. She met us at the door when we arrived home. Both she and Bruce inspected Jenny carefully. "She doesn't look too bad," Mother decided.

"No," Bruce agreed. "She's kind of cute."

Mother followed me upstairs to the nursery. She talked while I fed Jenny and put her to bed. "I've never seen a child as nervous as that Bruce. He paced the floor the whole time you were in labor. I didn't get a bit of sleep that night."

"I'm sorry, Mother. He worries."

"Too much, if you ask me."

"I know. I'll speak to him."

After Jenny fell asleep, I went looking for Bruce. I found him sitting on his bed petting Snook, the gray cat. I sat down and gave him a big hug. "Are you all right, Bruce?"

"Sure, Mom."

"You know everything's okay . You'll like having a sister."

He nodded. "I'll try."

Bruce seemed to relax then. We settled into a comfortable routine. John received another raise at work so we were relatively well off financially. I took care of the house and played with the children.

In September, Bruce started school. He would have to take the city bus. A few days before school started, I bundled Jenny into her buggy. We went with him to the bus stop. A cold wind blew dry leaves around. Shivers ran up my spine as I stood waiting with him until the bus arrived. Then a friendly driver reassured me. "Don't worry, I'll see that he gets off at the right stop."

"I'm going to meet him this first time." I rushed home, put Jenny in the car and drove to the place where Bruce would get off. We arrived just as the bus pulled up. The driver waved to me as Bruce stepped off.

Everything went smoothly for several weeks. Bruce seemed to enjoy school proudly bringing home crayon drawings and clay sculptures. Then one night I awoke to find him standing beside my bed. "What's wrong?" I mumbled sleepily.

"There's something in my room."

120

"Like what?"

"A MONSTER."

"There's no such thing. Come. I'll show you." I stumbled out of bed and walked with him to his room. I turned on the light. "See. There's nothing in here."

"Look under my bed."

I got down on the floor and looked. "Nothing." I pulled down the blankets for him. "Back to bed."

I covered him up. A few minutes later, he was in my room again.

"What now?"

"It's still there."

I sighed. "I'll come sit with you for a minute." I wanted to take him in bed with me. I had been taught that parents shouldn't do that. Instead, I wrapped a blanket around myself and followed him back to his room. I turned on the light again to show him that the room was empty. I sat on the foot of the bed and waited for him to fall asleep. It took a long time.

I was tired the next morning as I explained it to John.

He listened sympathetically. "This is an old house. Bruce probably heard the wind blowing through it. Don't worry, he'll sleep tonight."

"I hope so."

The next night, the same thing happened. "Come on, Bruce!" I cried "There's nothing is in your room."

"Yes, there is."

By the fourth night, I felt exhausted. "Neither of us can do our work." I complained to John.

"Why don't you call the doctor? Maybe he can give Bruce something. Then you can both sleep."

"Good idea."

The doctor listened unsympathetically. "Bruce is nervous about starting school. He's jealous of the new baby, too. You should insist that he stay in his own room. You're spoiling him."

"Okay. But could you give him something for a few nights so we can get some rest. We're really exhausted."

"Yes. For a few nights."

He called the drug store. I picked up the prescription. I was convinced that Bruce had heard something, so I bought rat traps, too. I baited some of the traps with cheese and some with peanut butter. I put them in the attic. "If there's anything up there, we'll catch it," I explained to Bruce. At bedtime, I gave him a dose of sleeping medicine. Both of us slept fine.

The next morning, I went up to the attic to check my traps. One of them had been sprung. I brought it down and showed it to Bruce. "Here's your monster, a squirrel. He's been inside the wall next to your bed."

He nodded. "I'm sorry it's dead. I wouldn't have been frightened if I'd known it was a squirrel."

That ended the sleeping problem, but a few months later, John needed his suitcase. When he went up to the attic to get it, he found it filled with acorns.

Chapter 10

"We're coming," Bruce answered. He climbed out of the tree house which John had built. Freddie and Timmy scrambled down behind him. All three crowded into my car. The boys had grown a good deal. Timmy, the tallest, had his mother's dark good looks.

I blew the horn of my red Corvair. "Hurry, boys. Don't take all day."

Blond Freddie seemed short by comparison, but with broad shoulders and strong legs. I was sure that he'd play football someday. Bruce looked like me with wavy brown hair and the family mole on his right cheek.

Three cub scouts, Jenny and I made quite a load. The boys loved my car. Bruce named it 'the lady bug'. He wanted to paint spots on it. I vetoed that idea.

He loved it, anyway. It became the official cub scout car. I was den mother and Jenny an was honorary member. Today we were going on a field trip. Loaded down with fishing poles, tackle and lots of food, we set out to catch ourselves a whale sized fish.

I drove to a wooded park on the edge of town. It had both fire rings for cooking and a quiet stretch of river. "What do you want to do first. Eat or fish?"

"Eat," they all cried.

"Okay. Hunt for firewood." I helped Jenny out of the car.

Bruce and Timmy set off to look for dry branches, but Freddie stood quietly watching me. His intense blue eyes followed my every move. I thought he must have something important on his mind, so I walked over to him. "What's wrong?"

"Nothing. I just wanted to show you something." He reached into his pocket and brought out a small can of insect repellent.

"What's it for?"

"It's to chase bugs away. I'm allergic to bees. The doctor told me that if I'm stung, I might die."

"That's serious. But there are no bees here. Put it away."

I reached in the picnic basket and drew out a small knife. "Here. You can cut green sticks to cook hot dogs on. Just be careful."

"Okay. Thanks."

Jenny and I unloaded our gear while Bruce built a fire. Soon the smell of roasted meat filled the air. I realized I was starving. My mouth watered as I handed buns to the boys. "Cook some for Jenny and me, will you, Bruce?"

"Sure, Mom. Here take this one." He handed me his. "I'll cook more."

"Thanks." I broke off a piece for Jenny.

After a few minutes, we were full and ready to fish. I gave the boys bright red bobbers to fasten on their lines. "If something takes your bait, the bobber will sink. When that happens, pull in your line."

They nodded. With our lines in the water, we all sat quietly. After a few minutes, something hit Timmy's bobber pushing it around in the murky water. "What was that?"

I shook my head. "I don't know."

"It wasn't a fish."

"It's a turtle," Bruce shouted. "See. There's one after my bobber now."

"You're right." A snapping turtle had attacked his float with its nose.

"Watch." Bruce pulled in his line. The turtle followed his bobber.

"Don't let it take your hook." I cautioned. "I'd never get that out."

"Let's catch it," Freddie cried.

"I want one, too." Jenny jumped up and down energetically. Her curly hair bounced in all directions.

"We each want one," Bruce added.

"Be careful not to hook them." I insisted. "Coax them in near shore. I'll pick them up in our net."

"What can we use for bait?"

"Try pieces of hot dog."

They all nodded. Catching turtles proved much more exciting than fishing. Before long, we had a bucket full.

"Okay, that's enough," I said. "Time to go home. Throw the turtles back in the river."

"Oh, Mom, can't we keep them?" Bruce pleaded.

"No. They belong here."

"Not even one?" Freddie asked.

"What would your mother say?"

"She won't mind. I'll take good care of it. I promise."

"It could be our mascot," Timmy suggested.

"You can keep one turtle. The rest go back in the river."

The boys nodded.

We packed up and headed for home. Freddie sat next to me proudly holding the turtle. When I turned onto our street he started to wiggle. "Let me out in the alley behind my house."

At first I didn't understand. "Where do you want me to let you off?"

"Behind the garage."

"Okay." I nodded laughing to myself.

As I drove up the alley, I passed Hannah, the elderly neighbor who lived behind me. She was busy working in her garden. She waved at us in a friendly way. "What have you all been up to?"

"Fishing."

"Catch anything?"

"Just this." Freddie held up the turtle.

"That's quite a catch."

A few days later I met Freddie walking home from school. "How is the turtle?"

He hung his head. "Mother wouldn't let me keep it. She made me take it down to the creek and let it go."

"Too bad." I shook my head. "Our cub scout den will have to find a new mascot. I have a black kitten named Inky. Would he do?"

"A cat's not as good as a turtle, but I guess he'd be okay."

"Good. It's settled."

Spring drifted into summer. It was time for our annual trip to Michigan. Things were different this year. Father had retired and built a new home on sand dunes overlooking Lake Michigan. His dark hair shown silver- gray in the sun light as he showed us around. I felt strange sitting in this new living room. It felt like being back in Minnesota. Father had built a scaled down version of Gray Tower.

The same pictures of stern faced ancestors stared down at us from heavy gold frames. My picture hung next to a huge stone fireplace which filled the room with aromatic warmth. In unguarded moments, I felt the presence of our old, familiar ghosts. Inside, nothing had changed.

Outside, the windswept dunes seemed as isolated and desolate as rural Minnesota had been. Father had managed to transplant his mood. Only one thing was missing. The stables were gone. Instead, Father had an extra garage for his garden tools and a miniature tractor. It came equipped with a little yellow wagon.

"You'll love this," he told Jenny as he backed it out. "Hop in. I'll give you a great ride."

Jenny laughed and scrambled in.

Mother stood nearby cutting roses. "Take her to see the vegetable garden," she suggested. "You can bring back something for our dinner."

Mother aged, too. Her hair had turned thin and white. The hands which loved to sew were now so stiff that she could barely cut roses. Arthritis in her knees made it difficult for her to reach the vegetable garden.

Father understood. "We have a lot vegetables growing," he told Jenny. "But no asparagus. The deer ate that. Too bad. It's your grandmother's favorite."

"It must be the deer's favorite, too."

"Never mind. We'll have carrots. You can help me pull them."

Father gunned his motor. They sped off at an alarming speed.

"Hang on, Jenny," I called after them.

"How far is that vegetable garden?" I asked Mother.

"Just over the hill. But he probably want's to show her the Christmas tree house first."

"What's that?"

We have a circle of pine trees growing close together. They look like one tree from a distance. If you walk inside the circle, you feel like you're in a house. Your father named it 'the Christmas tree house.' He took a picture of it to put on our Christmas cards."

"That'll be nice."

I followed Mother back into the kitchen. I helped her arrange flowers for the dining room table. After a few minutes Father's tractor bounced back over the dunes. I heard Jenny laughing and hurried outside.

Jenny was sitting in the back of the cart next to a mound of greens. "Look, Mommy." She held up a carrot. "We found this in the dirt. I pulled it out. Isn't that funny?"

"Yes. Lots of foods grow underground. Potatoes do and also peanuts. Come on, I'll help you down." I reached up to lift her.

Suddenly I felt a sharp pain in my side. I grabbed for my stomach as I doubled up.

"What's wrong?" Father asked as he climbed off the tractor.

"Just a little pain in my stomach. It'll go away. Don't worry."

"You were holding on to your stomach last night, too."

"A little indigestion. Jenny gets it, too."

"I don't like it. Promise me you'll both see the doctor when you get home."

" I'm sure it's nothing." I reached up and lifted Jenny out of the cart. "See. I'm fine now."

Jenny laughed. "You ought to see the Christmas tree house, Mommy. It's really big inside. We could sleep in there."

"Really! Maybe we'll do that. Bruce wanted to sleep outside."

Jenny jumped around excitedly. "Let's do it tonight."

"If your father approves. We'll talk at dinner. Run and wash up now."

I helped Father bring in the carrots. Soon, they were washed, cooked and ready to eat. Jenny carried them proudly to the dinner table. "I picked them all by myself. And then we went to the Christmas tree house. Can we sleep there tonight, Mommy? You promised."

"She wants to sleep out in a circle of trees, John. Is it all right?"

"Sounds great to me," Bruce added.

" I guess so." John turned to Mother. "Have you any old blankets that we could use."

Mother nodded. "I'll look."

Jenny wiggled excitedly.

Mother found a pile of old blankets left over from my brothers' camping days. "And a big piece of canvas, too," she added. "It'll keep you dry when the fog rolls in."

Father agreed. "I'll take you over in the cart. You won't

have to carry all these blankets."

"Can I ride with you?" Jenny asked.

"Sure. You want a ride, too, Bruce?"

Bruce shook his head. "I'm too big for that cart. I'll walk."

"I'll pack some snacks in case you get hungry," Mother offered.

"And I'll get our jackets," I added. " In case it gets cold."

We loaded everything into the cart. Jenny sat on a roll of blankets. The rest of us trailed along behind. Father gunned the tractor and shot out across the dunes. "Not so fast," I shouted into his dust. "We can't keep up."

"Sorry." Father slowed down a bit. At the Christmas tree house, he helped us unload our gear. "I'll be back in the morning," he promised.

"Better make it early," John said. "We haven't brought breakfast."

"Don't worry. I'll come at first light."

"What time is it now?" Bruce asked.

"About 8:00 PM. It stays light a long time in summer up here."

"Okay," John interrupted. "Let's get this stuff unloaded."

We carried our bedding into the circle of trees and spread it out on the ground. It was darker inside and harder to breathe. The air seemed heavy with the smell of pine.

We lay down on the canvas. Through a hole in the we trees, we watched the sky darken. One by one stars began to appear. A shooting star flashed past. "Make a wish," John said.

"What shall I wish for?" Jenny asked.

"Anything you want," Bruce answered. "But don't tell anyone. If you tell, it won't come true."

Jenny nodded. Then a long, wailing cry filled the air and she jumped. "What was that?"

"I think it was an owl," John replied .

"Or a mourning dove," I added.

"I think it was a wolf." Jenny shuddered.

Bruce laughed. "That's silly. There aren't any wolves around here."

"Yes, there are. Gramps said so."

"He was joking."

The sound came again, closer this time. Jenny started to cry. "I want to go home."

"It's nothing. Don't he afraid," her father reassured her.

" Please. Take me home."

"It's all right with me," Bruce said. "I'm bored anyway."

"And this ground is very hard," I added.

"How will we carry all this stuff?" John asked.

"We'll leave it here. Just wear our jackets. Father can pick the rest up in the morning. Nobody's going to steal it."

John stood up and put on his coat. I helped Jenny with hers. Then John took her hand. "Okay," he said. "I've got the flashlight."

Bruce and I followed him staying close to the light. We worked our way across the dunes.

"What are you doing back?" Father asked when he saw us.

"Jenny was frightened by an owl."

"It was a wolf."

"Or a mourning dove," Mother said. "They make strange night noises."

"Whatever it was, we're back."

"What time is it?" Bruce asked.

Father looked at his watch. "It's 9:30. Your camping trip lasted exactly an hour and a half"

"Long enough for me." I took Jenny's hand. "Come on. I'll give you a bath."

Chapter 11

Back in Wisconsin, I decided to take Father's advice and see my doctor. I still had pain in my right side. It was getting worse. I often spent half the night pacing the floor. It can't be my appendix, I thought, it's too high up. "Probably just gas," I told John. " But I should have it checked. I'd better take Jenny, too."

John nodded. "She always has a stomach aches. She comes to the table hungry. Then when she starts to eat, she cries."

"I know. I don't understand it. She has a fine red rash on her body, too. It comes and goes."

"Very strange. You'd definitely better take her with you."

A few days later, we went to the doctor. He looked us both over. "I think you have gall stones. I'd like you to have X-rays. I can't find anything wrong with Jenny. She's just imitating you."

"But she cries when she eats," I protested.

"Does she play hard?"

"Yes."

"She's not sick."

"I don't believe him," I told John. "But what more could I say?"

"Nothing, I guess. We'll just have to watch her carefully."

Next morning, I had to go the hospital for the X-rays. I asked Connie if she would watch Jenny.

"Sure. Unless it takes you all day."

"I'll be home by noon."

The hospital took longer than expected. It was after twelve when I returned. No one answered Connie's bell. I could hear voices so I walked around to the back. I arrived just in time to see our back alley neighbor, Hannah, spraying Jenny with an aerosol can. "What's that?" I asked.

"It's nothing. Just an insect repellent. Freddie is allergic to bug bites. His mother lets me put it on him. All the kids like it."

"You sprayed it on Jenny?"

"Sure. She likes it."

"I'd rather you didn't."

"She'll get bites."

"That's all right. She's not allergic to bugs."

But she might be allergic to that spray, I thought. It's the kind which caused me to break out when I was pregnant with her. I shook my head remembering the rash I had developed during our fishing trip. Jenny had the same kind of spots now. I took her hand. "Come on, Jenny. Time to go home."

Later Connie called on the phone. "What did your X-rays show?"

"Gall stones. The doctor wants to take them out."

"When will he do that?"

"In fall. After Jenny starts nursery school. I'll have more time."

"Can you wait that long?"

"The doctor gave me a diet. He told me not to eat egg yolks or fat."

"You're so thin now. You'll starve."

"I'll be okay. Thanks, for watching Jenny."

"Any time. And good luck with your food."

The diet proved more of a problem than I expected. Putting cottage cheese on my baked potato instead of butter seemed simple enough. John never noticed that I started frying hamburgers in water. That part worked fine. My stomach felt better.

The problem was weight loss. By August, I had turned into a skeleton. My doctor shook his head when he saw me. "You have to have that gall bladder out right now!"

I nodded. "But what about Jenny?" I had brought her with

132

me. Jenny was the one that I wanted him to see. "She still isn't eating. She's thinner than I am and has bruises all over like someone beat her."

I lifted her onto the examination table. "Show him your legs."

Jenny held them up.

"She has fever, too."

The doctor looked at her skeptically. "I'll order some tests. I don't expect to find anything."

"Thank you."

He called the next day with Jenny's test results. "She's a little anemic. I'll give her some iron. She'll be fine. I want you in the hospital for surgery immediately."

"Can't it wait until I'm sure Jenny's all right?"

"No. That gall bladder has to come out."

"Okay," I answered reluctantly.

My surgery proved routine. Soon I was on my feet and anxious to see Jenny. She hadn't responded to the iron treatment. She still cried at meals and the bruises were worse. Shortly after I returned home, her temperature shot up to over 104 degrees. I thought that children with anemia could have leukemia. Frantic! I called the doctor.

"Okay," he said. "I'll put her in the hospital for more tests."

I rushed her right down to the pediatric ward. The doctor called the next day. He sounded worried. Pain shot through my stomach when I heard his voice. "I want to see you and John in my office right away."

I called John at work. We rushed right over. When I saw the doctor, the look on his face confirmed my worst fears. "What is it, doctor? Leukemia?"

He shook his head. "I don't know. She doesn't have all the symptoms of leukemia. I can't make the diagnosis. She needs a specialist."

"What shall we do?"

"Could you take her to the Mayo clinic?"

"Of course."

The doctor nodded. "I'll make the arrangements. You should leave today."

Saint Mary's hospital in Rochester, Minnesota was an impressive, red brick building about two miles from the Mayo Clinic. John dropped Jenny and I at the emergency entrance before parking the car.

Jenny looked tired and pale. A nurse hurried her upstairs in a wheelchair. She was assigned to the sixth floor pediatrics unit. We saw children in wheelchairs speeding through the halls. They wore white cotton vests with long straps tied around the back of their chairs so they couldn't fall out.

They wore vests in bed, too. The straps were tied loosely to the sides of the cribs as a safety measure. This was a medical ward. Children here were less sick and consequently more active than those on other floors. I was happy that they had put Jenny here. It contained a big playroom with colored tables and chairs. Ambulatory patients could eat their meals here. Nurses held weekly parties for them. I admired nurses who could work with such sick children.

One nurse showed Jenny a crib in a pleasant room. "This will be your bed. The walls were plain with a large, sunny window. A happy rabbit holding flowers smiled from the end of the crib. Jenny hardly noticed. She was too tired and ill to care. I lifted her onto the bed and took off her shoes.

The nurse continued to talk. "This is your roommate, Cecelia," She said pointing to a little girl in the next bed. Cecelia was a small, dark skinned child with black curls and huge, bright eyes. She looked about three, a year younger than Jenny. She seemed healthy except for her lips and fingernails which were a strange blue color.

"She's come all the way from Australia, haven't you dear?"

"Yes." Cecilia seemed happy to have company. She grinned at Jenny. "Can you play?"

Jenny didn't answer. She sat quietly watching me remove her socks.

"Maybe later," I answered for her. "She's tired now."

John had stopped in admissions to do paper work. He now appeared in the doorway.

"Everything's taken care of. How do you feel, Jenny?"

"I want to go home. PLEASE, Mommy." She started to cry.

"We'll go home soon," John promised. First you have to get well."

"The doctors have to find out what's wrong with you," I added. "So they can make you better. You understand, don't you?"

Jenny wiped her nose with the back of her hand and nodded cautiously.

"That's my brave girl."

"Can I have a drink, Mommy?"

"I'll get you something," the nurse answered. "Would you like milk?"

"No, juice."

"Orange?"

"Tomato," I answered for her. "Orange upsets her stomach."

"I'll call downstairs for some."

"Me, too, Mommy," Cecilia said looking at me.

"Can she have some, too?"

"Yes. I'll call down two orders."

I was surprised that she had called me "Mommy," so I followed the nurse out into the hall. "Where's Cecilia's Mother?"

"She's an orphan. Some church group raised money to send her here. She has a serious condition."

"She couldn't come alone?"

"A foster mother brought her. The woman doesn't spend much time with Cecelia." The nurse shook her head. "She sits in the smoking lounge."

"Too bad. Cecelia's such a sweet child."

The nurse nodded.

Cecilia was a wonderful roommate, always cheerful. She loved any game we could devise. She called me "Mommy" and John "go smoke" because every once in a while he'd say, "I guess I'll go out for a smoke."

Cecilia helped to counteract the endless flow of medical personnel which came to examine Jenny. They looked at the chart, examined her, and then turned to me with the question, "Have you other children?"

"I have a son at home."

"Good."

I heard that same question so often that it began to get on my nerves. I didn't like the implication.

The doctors were trying hard to diagnose her. They ran endless tests. One day they took a sample of bone marrow. "After we get these results, we'll be able to transfuse her," they told me. "That should make her feel better."

"I hope so."

John and I met Cecilia's foster mother in the smoking lounge. She was a large black woman, named Mary, who seemed anxious to leave. "When I get home, I'm going to sleep for a week," she told us.

"Can't you sleep here?"

"No. It's hard to sleep in a strange bed. I miss my own things."

I nodded. "Will you be here long? What's wrong with Cecilia?"

"She was born without the valves which keep her blood

moving in the right direction. The doctors are trying to find a way to fix that."

"Sounds difficult to me."

" I hope it won't take long." She stood up "I'd better check her."

When we were alone, I turned to John. "That woman bothers me. All she can talk about is going home."

"That's understandable. Why does it upset you?"

"Because she said, 'when I go home,' not, 'when WE go home'."

John nodded. "It did sound like she planned go alone."

Back in the room, my heart sank when I saw poor Jenny. Someone had started her transfusion. She lay perfectly still, but with a troubled look on her pale face.

"What's wrong, pumpkin?" John asked. "Does that hurt?"

"No. But they promised me tomato juice. No one has brought it."

I pointed to the sack of blood. "I think they may have meant that."

Jenny shook her head. "That's not tomato juice."

John heading for the door. "I'll see if I can find you some."

"Me too," Cecelia called.

"I'll do my best."

On the way back from the nurses station, John met Jenny's hematologist, a small, nervous man with a wind tanned face. "I want to speak to you and your wife in the lounge."

John nodded and went to get me. "Your juice will be here in a minute," he told the girls. He turned to me. "Come have a smoke."

Pain shot through my stomach when I saw his face. I nodded and went with him. The doctor was waiting. "Your daughter has aplastic anemia."

"What's that?" "Something has poisoned her bone marrow.

She isn't making blood.Her platelets are especially low.That's why we are giving her whole blood."

"Can you cure her?"

"Maybe. If we find the cause. We won't give up hope."

I didn't like the sound of his reply. "What can we do?"

"Make a list of every chemical in your house. Mail it to me. Then throw them all away. Particularly benzene ring compounds."

"Okay."

"She'll feel better with fresh blood in her. I want to start some medication, too. If she tolerates it, she can go home."

"That's wonderful."

Jenny handled the medication. A few days later the doctor told us we could leave. John and I went to say good-bye to Mary. "Have you any idea how long you'll be here?" I asked.

"They're going to operate on Cecelia. I'll be here a while longer."

"I hope her surgery's a success so you can both go home."

She gave a long sigh. "Thank you."

Back home, our black cat, Inky, became Jenny's constant companion. He would jump onto the bed and curl up beside her. I'd better keep him inside for the next couple of weeks, I thought. Sometimes people hurt cats this close to Halloween. Jenny looked pale next to the black cat. Her skin was so white that it seemed opaque.

She was terribly ill again. I expected her doctor to call any minute with the results of her latest blood tests. I didn't have to wait long before the phone rang. "She's bad," the voice on the phone said. "We couldn't find any platelets at all. She needs another transfusion."

"I'll bring her into the hospital."

"It would be better to take her back to Rochester. They have a platelet separator."

"Okay."

"You'll have to fly. We don't have an air ambulance. I've arranged a charter flight."

"Is it that urgent?"

"Yes. The weather is getting bad. You have to leave within the hour."

"I'll get her ready."

I called John at work and explained the situation. He let me finish, then spoke quietly, his voice heavy with fear. "I'll stop at the bank. Then drive you to the airport."

We took off an hour later. "I want to come, too," John said as he lifted Jenny into the back of the plane beside me.

The pilot, Neil, shook his head. He had a kind face, tanned and deeply furrowed. "You stay home with your son." He waved at a man standing nearby. "Curly's coming with us. Don't worry. We'll take care of them."

Jenny fell asleep in my arms. I held her close as we flew deeper and deeper into dense clouds. Rain pelted the windows obstructing my view. Every few minutes Neil would dip down close to the ground while Curly peered out the window, looking for landmarks.

We passed a water tower with a name on it. I saw a road and realized that we were flying in circles, trying to land. My heart sank. I felt terribly guilty. These men were endangering their lives for us. They had families of their own. I had no right to ask them to take such a risk for a child as sick as Jenny. She was my problem, not theirs. I had no time to think about it. Neil saw a hole in the clouds, gunned the engine, and burst through into sunlight. We touched down on a runway. Safe at last!

As soon as the plane stopped, Curly jumped out, picked Jenny up and ran for the terminal. I followed panting. Neil brought the luggage. In front of the terminal, I saw a bus loading passengers from a jet which had landed just ahead of us. The men bundled Jenny and I on board. "Will you drive them to the hospital?" Curly asked.

The driver looked at Jenny and nodded. "I'll take them straight to the emergency entrance."

"Aren't you coming, too?" I asked.

Curly shook his head. "We have to stay with the plane."

I nodded.

"Thank you." I called back as the bus pulled away.

Someone must have called ahead. A nurse with a wheelchair was waiting at the door when we arrived. Gratefully, I lifted Jenny down from the bus and into that chair.

"Don't forget your suitcases." The driver handed them down.

"Thanks. What do I owe you?"

"No charge. And don't worry. They'll take care of her. Mayo's the best."

"I know."

He waved good-bye. I picked up our suitcases and followed the nurse. She went right by admitting and straight into the elevator. Inside, she turned to me. "Do you have other children at home?"

My heart sank. I had heard that question too many times before. "Yes. I have a son."

"Good."

The door opened. We stepped out into the pediatric ward. The whole floor had been decorated for Halloween. Every door had a bright cardboard pumpkin taped to it. I saw yellow and black balloons in the playroom as we passed.

Jenny seemed oblivious to it all. Our nurse wheeled her to an empty room. I lifted her into bed. As I pulled the cover over her, she closed her eyes and fell asleep.

"We've had her records sent up." the nurse explained "Her

doctor is looking at them. He'll be in to talk to you in a minute."

I nodded.

There was nothing more I could do. I walked down the hall quietly glancing into every room. I was looking for Cecilia. She wasn't there. I knew she should still be in the hospital if her surgery had been successful. There was only one other possibility. I didn't want to think about that. Poor little Cecilia. She would be missed.

Sadly, I turned and headed back towards Jenny's room. I found a doctor reading her chart.

"She's bad again." I told him.

"So I see. I want another bone marrow test. After that, we'll give her some platelets."

"Why don't you give her whole blood?"

"She doesn't need it. She's less apt to develop an allergic reaction to platelets alone."

"I see."

"Have you cleaned your house and removed everything which might be toxic to her?"

"Yes. I did as you told me. I made a list for you. Then I threw out everything but plain soap and the fly swatter."

He nodded. " Here's the list." He glanced through it. "Nothing here seems to be very toxic. Are you sure this is everything?"

Suddenly I remembered the rash which I had while I was pregnant with her. It was similar the spots Jenny had after Hannah sprayed her. "Could insect repellent cause this?"

"Possibly. We don't know for sure."

After the doctor left, I sat with Jenny waiting for her to wake up. The room was hot. I felt exhausted. I must have dozed. The sound of her voice woke me. "Mommy, I'm thirsty."

"What would you like to drink?"

"Tomato juice."

"I'll ask the nurse to bring you some."

"I'm sorry," she said when she heard what we wanted, "It's too close to dinner. Everyone in the kitchen is busy preparing trays. They haven't time to get it right now."

Jenny started to cry.

"Is there someplace nearby where I could buy some?"

"The doctors' lounge. They have a drink machine."

"How do I find it?"

"Take the elevator to the basement. Then left at the end of the hall."

"Thanks." I turned to Jenny. "I'll find you some."

"Okay, Mommy. But come right back."

"I will." I headed for the elevator. When it stopped in the basement, I stepped out into an empty, seemingly endless hall. Each step I took echoed against the bare walls. I hope I don't come to the morgue, I thought.

I was dizzy. The walls seemed to close in around me. Every step felt like I was walking through glue. My heart pounded. I fought to breathe. I forced myself to put one foot in front of the other. Slowly, I inched down that hall. At last, I saw a door. The doctors' lounge. I'd made it! I found a room with comfortable sofas and brightly colored chairs. The air smelled of strong coffee and stale smoke. I located the vending machine and soon had a can of juice for Jenny and coffee for myself. Thank goodness! It had been a long, hard day.

Chapter 12

Jenny died on December 13th, 1960 just three months before her fifth birthday. She died of transfusion reaction. December had turned bitterly cold. When she became critical again, we decided to transfuse her at our local hospital.

"It's up to you," her doctor told John and me. "There is nothing more they can do for her at Mayo. We can give her whole blood just as easily here."

I agreed. "I see no point in subjecting her to that long, cold trip."

John nodded. It was decided.

She died on Friday the thirteenth. My parents flew up from Florida for the service. They acted surprised by her death. After Father retired, they traveled most of the time. Out of touch with us, they hadn't understood the seriousness of her illness. Now they joined us on a barren hill and watched as strangers lowered her into frozen ground.

Bruce stood ramrod stiff beside me. "I wish it would snow. She's too little to lie there in that frozen dirt. Snow would at least spread a clean, white blanket over her."

I nodded, understanding. "She isn't alone you know. She has a friend in Heaven."

"You mean God?"

"Of course she has God. But she has someone else, too."

"Who?" Bruce asked cheering up a little.

"She has a friend from Mayo named Cecilia."

"Good. I'm glad she's not alone. She won't be so frightened if she has someone."

I took his hand. Together we walked back towards the car. We reached it just as it started to snow. Bruce stopped, looked up at the sky and whispered, "Thanks, Cecilia."

****

My steps echoed in the empty house. I felt as though the heart had been torn out of me leaving a giant hole. It was as though the child in me died with Jenny. Only the shell of an adult remained. But that person had one last task to do for her.

Jenny's room was filled with beautiful toys which friends sent during her illness. With Christmas only days away, I decided to give them to the poor.

Slowly, I walked down the hall to her room. Inky, her black cat, followed close behind. He stopped short when he saw the empty room. Normally, he would have jumped onto her bed. This time, he sat near the door and watched me. I put all her toys into a large box. I folded each piece of clothing carefully before adding it to the box. Finally, I took the bedding from Jenny's bed and carried it out to the laundry. Inky followed. He watched as I put her sheets into the washer. Then he turned and went back to her empty room. Sitting in the doorway, he started to cry. I couldn't believe it! I had never heard a cat make that noise before.

"Stop that, Inky."

He looked at me for a moment, then resumed howling.

"Do you need to go out?" I picked him up and carried him outside. Inky circled the yard slowly. He smelled every blade of grass. He didn't stop crying. He sounded even louder .

"Can't you do something about that cat?" John asked when he arrived home from work.

"I've tried. Nothing works. He cries when he's indoors and even louder when I let him out."

"Lock him in the basement."

"That would be cruel. I think he's grieving. He misses Jenny."

"She was in the hospital many times. He didn't act like this."

"It's different now. He knows."

"That's impossible. He's just a cat."

"Maybe. But he started crying when I emptied her room. He knows that she isn't coming back."

"Nonsense."

"Then you explain it."

"I can't."

Inky cried for days until one morning I noticed that he was limping. I took him to the vet. "He has an abscess in his right side. I'll give him a shot of antibiotics. You should put warm compresses on him."

"Okay."

After a few days of compresses, a big hole opened up in Inky's side. I took him back to the vet. The doctor examined him again. "There's a bullet in there. Someone's shot him with a pellet rifle."

I'm not surprised, I thought. He made so much noise. One of the neighbors decided to quiet him with a gun. "Can you take it out?"

"No. It's too close to his spine. But the infection has drained. I think he'll get well. Don't worry. Your cat will be fine."

"Thank goodness!"

Back home, I lifted Inky onto my bed and sat beside him. I stroked him gently being careful not to touch his sore. My shoulders shook. A torrent of tears poured from my eyes. "You're not the only one with a hole inside," I told him. "I have one, too. And mine will take a long time to heal."

Chapter 13

I stood at my window watching the little girl playing school with a bucket full of frogs. She was about five years old with ash-blond hair pulled back in a pony tail. The pink ribbon in her hair exactly matched her lightweight, summer slacks.

She had a charming laugh. I had heard her laughing earlier while Bruce helped her catch frogs. She wasn't laughing now. Patiently, she took each frog out of the bucket and placed it on the picnic table. She wanted them all to sit in a straight line. But as soon as she had three or four of them lined up, one would jump off. As she hurried to catch it, another would hop away.

I admired her tenacity. She kept trying for at least half an hour. Finally, she ran out of frogs. They had all escaped. She shook her head sadly. She picked up the bucket and headed back toward the creek where Bruce sat fishing, "Bruce," she called, "will you catch more frogs? Mine are all gone."

"Not now, Linda. I'm trying to catch a fish."

She nodded. "I'll catch one, too."

"You don't have a pole."

"I'll use yours."

"All right. Come here and I'll show you how."

I smiled. Bruce had changed in the last few months. He had grown tall and strong. He had matured emotionally as well. How patient he was with Linda. He acted much older than ten. This was the same stream which he had fished with his cub scouts. They had light heartedly caught turtles. Now, in August of 1961, he was serious as he taught this child to fish.

We were staying in a little cottage next to a motel while we built a new home. Our old house had been sold. This place belonged to the motel's owners. Linda was their daughter.

"We don't ordinarily let her associate with motel guests,"

Linda's mother explained. "It's too dangerous. But you're different. You're local people, members of our church. It will be okay if she plays with Bruce."

"Thank you," I answered. "I'll keep a close eye on her."

It hurt me to watch Linda play. She was so vibrant, so alive. Once Jenny had been like that. Now she was gone, leaving a huge, aching hole inside me. Bruce and John must have holes inside, too, I realized.

I'll just have to have another baby, I decided. No one could take Jenny's place. But with another baby, we could make a new place. We'd start over with a new child for our new house.

I hadn't really wanted to build the house. Mother had persuaded me. She talked me into it. "It will give you something new to think about. It'll take your mind off Jenny."

She was wrong. The house had been designed before Jenny died. Every board was a painful memory. I knew Father wanted us to build it. Doing so would make us look prosperous. That would make the company look good. I did it to please Father.

Maybe a new baby would help, I thought. The child would be a lot younger than Bruce, but he might not mind. After all he's playing with Linda. Yes. I'll get pregnant, I decided as I turned away from the window.

We stayed in the cottage until Labor Day, then we moved into the new home. It was a split level ranch house tucked into a hill high above the high school football field. Bruce and John could sit in our living room and watch games being played below.

"That's no fun," John complained to me. "We want to sit in the stands, eat hot dogs and root for our team like everybody else."

"Go ahead. Just don't complain when you can't find a parking place."

We moved into the house before it was finished. The guest

bedroom and bath still needed painting. All of the landscaping remained undone.

"I'll supervise the gardeners myself and plant all the flower," I promised John. It didn't work out that way.

In early November, I started bleeding and made a hasty trip to the doctor. The same outspoken obstetrician who had delivered Jenny, soon confirmed my fears. "You are pregnant, but you never really recovered from the gall bladder operation. You're exhausted and much too thin. You'll have to be very careful if you want to carry this baby."

"What should I do?"

"Nothing."

"What?"

"I mean it. You are to do nothing but rest."

"How can I do that?"

"You'll manage. Stay away from wet paint, too."

I sighed.

I kept my word. When the painters arrived, I moved into a hotel near Bruce's school. Still bleeding, I spent my time in bed making small gifts which John delivered to our pediatric ward. Bruce walked over from school every day to have lunch with John and me. I ordered food from room service which was ready when my men arrived. It was a strange arrangement. Thank goodness, it didn't last long. The paint dried so I could go home.

"You still have to be quiet," the doctor warned at my next visit. "The holidays are coming. You are going to ignore them. No parties. No entertaining. And absolutely no shopping! Understand?"

"Yes, sir." I knew I had to follow his advice.

I spent my time in bed reading Christmas catalogs and wrapping small gifts for hospitalized children. I hired someone to clean and help with the cooking. She was a strong, competent farm woman whom we called Mrs. B. She usually came on Friday. Thanksgiving week she decided to come on Wednesday instead. "That way I can fix you a nice turkey."

"Thank you."

"You need fattening up and so does that baby."

"I'll work on it."

On Wednesday, a business associate sent us a fresh twenty-four pound turkey. Mrs. B. laughed when she saw it. "I'll stuff it and put it right in the oven. You can eat it tonight. I'll make a pumpkin pie, too."

"You're spoiling me."

"Never mind. It's for the baby."

Before long the house filled with the wonderful odor of roasting meat. Besides turkey, Mrs. B fixed vegetables, rolls and cranberry sauce.

"Dinner smells wonderful," Bruce said when he arrived home from school. "When do we eat?"

"As soon as your father arrives."

John was equally delighted. "Let's use the good dishes and really make it a celebration. "It's the first holiday in our new home."

I agreed.

We had just finished eating when our doorbell rang. "Who could that be?" John asked as he went to see. He opened the door and gasped. There stood Mr. and Mrs. Ryan, a couple of Father's oldest friends.

"Hello, John," Mr. Ryan said. "Nice to see you again."

I recognized his voice and hurried to the door. I liked these people. I had known them most of my life. Mr. Ryan had just retired. He was in the process of moving to Florida, so I was amazed to see these frail, gray haired people shivering on my doorstep. "What are you doing here?"

"You look surprised," Mrs. Ryan said as she stepped into

our front hall. "Weren't you expecting us?"

"No."

"Didn't your parents tell you? They invited us here for a meeting."

"Tonight?" I couldn't believe it.

"Tomorrow. Your brother and his wife will be here, too."

"On Thanksgiving?"

"Yes. There will be six of us."

"I'm glad we've got a big turkey. Have you had dinner?"

"We ate at the hotel. But we could use some coffee. It's cold outside."

I waved toward the living room ."I'll get some. Come in and sit down."

John took their coats. I hurried to bring coffee. "How about some pumpkin pie?" I called from the kitchen.

"Just coffee, thanks."

We talked to the Ryans until midnight. They explained that Father wanted Mr. Ryan to help reorganize a small company which he had bought in Florida. Father hoped it would keep them both busy during their retirement. Father would be C.E.O. My older brother, Sam, would take control if something happened to him.

"Why are you meeting at my house?"I asked Mother the next day as I stood in the kitchen slicing cold turkey.

"You live halfway between the Ryans' house in Minnesota and Sam's home in Wisconsin. Besides, I wanted to take care of you."

I shook my head. Bringing me six guests for Thanksgiving dinner wasn't my idea of caring. I never could understand Mother.

Although I made it through the weekend, I was thankful when Sunday night arrived and everyone left.

"How do you feel?" John asked as we undressed for bed.

"Tired."

"Any bleeding?"

"A little."

"You stay in bed tomorrow. Don't do a thing."

"I won't."

I kept my word. It wasn't good enough. At my next appointment, the doctor was even more insistent. "You're partially dilated," he explained. "You must stay in bed. All THE TIME."

"I will. I promise."

John had to carry my meals upstairs. For Christmas, he bought me a record of the musical *Camelot.* I spent hours listening to the bitter sweet melodies. In February, as snow lay deep outside our door, I started to bleed heavily. My heart pounded with fear for the baby as an ambulance rushed me to the hospital.

I was in labor much too soon! I had carried the baby for only 26 weeks. My doctor hurried into the delivery room. "It has a chance," he explained. "Babies have been born this early and survived."

"I hope so." I gasped as a contraction took my breath away. The anesthesiologist put something over my face. Overwhelmed by pain, I fought to breath. I wanted more air than the mask allowed. I shook my head trying to shake the mask off. It wouldn't budge.....

Sometime later I felt the light. My delivery room seemed dim by comparison. It was as though someone had opened a door at the end of a hall. The light which poured through was so intense that I knew I could not look at it.

I watched the scene in the delivery room from a vantage point near the ceiling. I had an excellent view of myself on the table as I struggled to deliver this premature baby. An anesthesiologist hovered near my head. At the other end of the table, my doctor stood ready for the delivery.

It seemed perfectly natural to watch from a spot just below the ceiling. Being outside my body was acceptable.Then the light appeared and with it a voice."Choose," the voice commanded. The word tore at my heart.

I wanted my dead daughter back. I yearned for my family to be whole again. That couldn't be. I had to choose whether to follow my daughter into the brilliant light or stay behind with my husband and son.

I thought that if I decided to go, the baby which I was delivering would live, staying behind with my men. But if I decided to remain with them, the baby would die. It would take a tiny part of me up into that light to be with my lost daughter.

"Choose," the voice said again, and I knew that I had to stay with my husband and son. They, too, had suffered a great loss. I could not add to their pain by leaving them.

I looked down and saw my doctor holding a baby. Suddenly, I was back in my body. The brilliant light had vanished. My doctor spoke to me. "I don't know whether she was born alive or dead. I'm going to baptize her. Are you Catholic or Protestant?"

"Protestant. It's a girl?"

"Yes. Do you want to name her?"

"No. I guess not."

He nodded and turned away to perform the ritual.

Tears burned my eyes. She would have been called Sheila if she'd lived. But she doesn't need a name now. She has a different destiny. This baby will carry my love to my other daughter, the one whom I miss so desperately.

Chapter 14

A robin sang in an elm tree near the park bench where I sat waiting on a cold spring day in 1963. I felt grateful for company. The park was empty except for us. We were both waiting for our mates. I hoped mine would come soon. He had been inside the Wisconsin State Adoption Agency for nearly an hour. The social worker had talked to me first. She was a stern, middle aged woman dressed in a no-nonsense business suit. My heart fell when I saw her.

"Why do you want to adopt a child?" she asked as soon as I sat down.

"Because my doctor told me that I shouldn't have more pregnancies."

She already knew the answer. She had my application in front of her. She studied it for a moment. "You have a natural born son."

"Yes. I want to adopt a daughter."

The woman pointed to my application and frowned. "It says here that you lost a natural daughter. Is that true?"

"Yes. She was four."

"And now you want to adopt a baby?"

"No. I want an older child. Someone big enough to play with my son."

The woman stiffened. "We don't usually place children with couples who already have a natural child."

My stomach twisted into a tight knot. The woman seemed so cold, so heartless. "Please try. I don't want my son to grow up alone." I paused searching for words to persuade her. "I would be a good mother to a girl."

"Now you can give all of your love to the boy. Do you think you could share that love with a strange child?"

I thought for a moment. I had to choose my words carefully. "Love isn't something which you divide like pie. I have loved many different people, loved each of them with all of my heart. I would have to divide my time between the two children, not my love."

"This child could never take your dead daughter's place."

Her words tore at my heart. "I know," I whispered. "No one could do that. But for a new child, I would make a new place."

"Good!" Her face softened. "I'll see what I can do."

Outside, I traded places with John. Now he was inside talking while I waited anxiously in the park. As I paced up and down nervously, a flock of chickadees landed nearby. They paid no attention to me, just chattered as they searched nearby trees for bugs.

Watching them, I relaxed. Everything's going to be all right, I told myself. I waited for a long time. At last, John arrived. He looked exhausted, but he had a huge smile on his face. "We qualified. They're going to find us a little girl."

My heart sang as I thought about the little girl we would soon adopt. The bedroom across the hall from mine would be perfect for her. We painted the walls a light gray with dresser and desk to match. I found fabric in a gray and rose pattern and made draperies. I bought bright rose material for a bedspread and to upholster an antique chair which my grandmother had given me.

Someone from the adoption agency would inspect our house to make sure it was suitable for a child. "They'll think it's perfect," I told John.

"It is nice. When will the social worker come?"

"Soon, I hope."

The inspector arrived a few days later. He paid little attention to my decorating. He wanted to see fire exits and working plumbing. Slowly he circled the house making notes on a clip board. Finally. he arrived back at the front door. He stop writing and looked at me. "Yes. It'll do."

I was overjoyed. His approval was the last thing we needed to qualify for the adoption. I waited excitedly. Every time the phone rang I thought it would be the agency saying that they had found us a little girl. Unfortunately, the call which changed our lives proved different.

Mother called to say that Father had been admitted to a hospital in Minneapolis. "He has cancer but he won't believe it. He thinks that he's had an automobile accident." She stopped speaking for a moment overwhelmed with tears. Then she whispered, "Come right away."

"I'll be there tomorrow."

John helped me pack and drove me to the airport. Soon, I found my myself hurrying down another long white hall toward a sterile hospital room. Inside, Father looked frail and troubled. He raised his head slowly to speak to me. His voice sounded heavy from drugs. "Good. I'm glad you weren't hurt in the wreck. How's Sam? Is he all right?"

For a moment I couldn't answer. What was he asking? How could discuss an accident which had never occurred. I thought frantically before I replied. "He's fine. You were the only one hurt."

"Thank God!" He smiled and relaxed, dropping into sleep. I decided to have a cup of coffee. In the hall, I met Doctor Grosse. He looked much older than I remembered him and very worried. "Have you seen your father?"

"Yes. He seemed groggy. Is he getting a lot of medication?"

Doctor Grosse nodded. "Your father's in a great deal of pain."

"I've heard that pain medication can becomes ineffective in cancer patients. What will you do if that happens?"

"I don't know. It's a serious problem and even more so in

your father's case. He doesn't want to stay here. He's determined to go back to his house in Michigan."

"Is that possible?"

"Not if he needs this much medication. We have to monitor it."

I hesitated, thinking. "When I was at Mayo with Jenny, I heard of a treatment for cancer. Doctors used Xray to deadened the pain carrying nerves. After that, the patient didn't need so much medication."

"There is such a treatment. It's used on terminally ill patients."

"Would it help Father?"

"Maybe. I'll find out."

"Thank you."

A few days later, Dr. Grosse again met me in the hall. "I've checked on the Xray treatment. It could be used on your father. He might have a slight limp afterwards, but it should stop the pain."

"Good. Let's do it."

"We need your mother's consent."

"I have to leave tomorrow, so you'll have to explain it to her. I'm sure she'll give you permission."

He nodded. "I'll take care of it."

"Thanks, again," I repeated gratefully.

I flew home the next day relieved to know that they could make Father's last days comfortable.

Later, Mother called say that the Xray treatment had been successful. She and Father were returning to Michigan.

"That's wonderful," I replied. But I knew it would be hard on her. Fortunately, she managed to find nurses. I flew over whenever I could.

Bruce went with me. Summer had arrived so he was out of school. There were no commercial planes into the small local airport. I called Neil, the pilot who had flown Jenny and I to Mayo.

At the airport, Neil looked at me and shook his head. "Just once, I'd like to take you someplace when it wasn't an emergency." He turned to Bruce and smiled. "You sit up front with me. I'll teach you to fly."

Bruce beamed. "Oh boy! Thanks."

For the next couple of hours, I couldn't be sure who was flying the plane. Sometimes I thought it flew itself, but I felt grateful to Neil for making Bruce happy. I knew he wouldn't have much fun this summer.

We made the trip several times. Each time I returned to my parents home I was amazed at how much it resembled the house in Minnesota which had frightened me as a child.

It seemed as though Father had taken the spirit of that house and set it down on this isolated hill in Michigan. Wind whistled in through the chimney while stern faced ancestors stared down, intimidating me. I shook my head. I was still living in the shadow of Gray Tower. Would I ever be really free of it?

Father had little pain now, but was extremely restless. He wandered around the house at all hours. Mother found a young medical student who was free for the summer. He kept an eye on Father at night while the rest of us slept. He respected Father for his tenacity and courage. I was thankful to this student for being there. I worried less when I had to leave.

One day, while I was at home, a social worker called. "We've found a little girl for you. She's two years old."

"That young?" I had expected someone older. "You said we would receive an older child."

The social worker laughed. "Children older than one year are older children to us. Do you want to meet her?"

My heart pounded. I felt excited and worried at the same time. "Of course. But we have a problem."

"What's that?"

"My father's dying. He could go any time."

"We'd better wait. It wouldn't be fair to the child to place her in your home right now."

"Will that be all right? Can we wait?"

"It's not a problem. She's in a foster home. Call me when you're free."

"Thank you." I felt relieved and gratefully.

On August thirteenth, Mother called to say that Father was back in the hospital. He was unconsciousness and not expected to recover.

I called John. We flew back as quickly as possible, but arrived too late. He was gone. We buried Father on a wind-swept hill in Michigan which is where he wanted to be.

****

I hadn't felt close to Father during his lifetime so I was amazed by my deep feeling of loss when he died. I played the theme song from the movie, High Noon over and over again. "Do not forsake me, oh my darling" went the song. I played it for days. Finally, a phone call in late September jolted me out of my depression.

"Are you ready to meet your prospective daughter ?" the voice on the phone asked.

"Oh, yes."

"She's two years old and living in a foster home about fifty miles north of you. Could you and your husband drive up there to meet her?"

"Certainly." My heart pounded with excitement.

"How would next Wednesday be?"

"I'll have to check with John, but I'm sure it'll be fine."

"We don't want the foster parents to know where she's going, so you'll meet our agent, Mr. Nally, at his office. He'll drive you out to her house. Is that satisfactory?"

"Of course. Can we bring our son, Bruce?"

"No, I wouldn't do that just yet. We want you to make three visits to get acquainted before you bring the child home. It would be better if just you and your husband came the first couple of times."

"All right. Can you tell me her name."

"Her name's Molly."

"That's a nice name. I can hardly wait to meet her."

"Good, we'll see you Wednesday at one o'clock"

"It's a date."

John and Bruce were excited when I told them. Bruce thought he should be able come. "She's going to be my sister. I should be able to check her out, too."

"Don't worry, you'll get a chance," John promised. "We won't bring her home until after you've met her."

"Promise. You won't forget?"

"Never."

I awoke Wednesday, to a beautiful, fall day. The sun shone brightly. The air felt cold with promise of frost. One o'clock seemed like an eternity to wait. Finally, the morning passed.

"Let's start early so we'll have plenty of time to find the agent's office," I begged John. "I don't want to be even one minute late."

"Don't worry. We won't be."

He kept his word. At exactly one o'clock we walked into the adoption agent's office. He was waiting for us, a short man in a shiny blue suit.

"Mr. Nally?" John asked.

"Yes. Won't you come in?" He ushered us into his small office and sat down opposite us. Opening a file on his desk, he read it to us. " The child is a Caucasian girl, born on May 1st, 1961 to a sixteen year old mother." He looked up at us and smiled. " The mother had red hair. I'm telling you this in case the child ever asks about her mother."

He searched through the file. "I don't seem to have any physical description of the father but Molly had pneumonia and a serious penicillin reaction. Other than that, she seems healthy." He paused and looked at us. "Do you want to meet her?"

"Oh, yes."

"Good. Let's get started." He stood up and headed towards the door. We drove a short distance out of town to a low white bungalow with a wide porch across the front. In back, we could see an unmowed grassy lawn with a swing set and a sand box. Beyond the yard, a high fence separated it from a railroad track. A good thing, I thought with children in the yard.

As soon as our car stopped, the front door opened and a wiry, gray haired woman came out. She smiled a warm greeting. "Come in, come in. "

"Thank you."

We saw a little girl peeking through a bedroom door. She had a little round face, huge blue eyes and straw colored hair with just a touch of red in it. She wore pink overalls and a long sleeved white turtle neck.

The front of her hair had been pulled back and fashioned into one long curl down the back of her head. In her hand, she held a worn pink monkey. She looked scared to death. I wanted to pick her up and comfort her. But I thought that would frighten her more so I just smiled.

"Please, sit down," offered the woman pointing to a couch. She turned to the child, "Come here, Molly, don't be afraid."

Molly came slowly into the room. She stopped beside her foster mother. She stood silently staring at us. I thought she would feel more comfortable if I ignored her for the moment. I spoke to the woman instead. "Is she allergic to anything besides penicillin?"

"Yes, she can't drink orange juice. I've been giving her grape drink."

I nodded, "That's good to know. Anything else?"

Mr. Nally shuffled his feet and coughed impatiently. So I turned my attention to Molly. "Hi Molly. Would you show me your swing?" She nodded and dropped her pink monkey.

I took her hand. We walked out into the yard. "Would you like me to push you?"

She raised her arms so I could pick her up. "Push me high."

We played for a few minutes, then went back into the house. To my surprise, John and Mr. Nally were at the door preparing to leave. It had been a very short visit.

"Bye, Molly," I called as I got into the car.

"Bye," she answered waving.

"Do you want her? Mr. Nally asked as we drove away.

"Yes," I answered.

"And you?" he asked John.

"Certainly. But it wasn't much of a visit."

"You can stay longer tomorrow."

"Tomorrow?" I repeated not expecting the next visit so soon.

"Yes, certainly. We don't like these things to drag out." He sounded very businesslike. "Tomorrow you are to bring your own car. I want you to invite her to go for a ride. That way she can get used to going with you. It will be easier when you take her home."

"Okay."

The next afternoon John took the initiative. Soon after we arrived he smiled at Molly. "Would you like to go for a ride in our car? We could buy you some ice cream."

Molly shook her head.

"She likes to wait for the school bus," her foster mother

explained. "She misses the other children now that school has started."

"We could ride around in the car and look for the school bus," John suggested. "Would you like that?"

Molly glanced at her foster mother who nodded her approval.

"I guess so."

She didn't sound to sure so I added, "We could buy ice cream, too."

"I'd like that."

The foster mother walked out to the car with us. She took Molly's hand and put it in mine.

"Come on, Molly," I reassured her. "We'll have fun."

I lifted her onto my lap and we set off. Every time we stopped at a stop sign John would say, "Look for the school bus."

We looked right and left, but never saw a bus. It was too early in the afternoon. We found an ice cream store where we bought Molly a cone.

"What kind do you like?" John asked.

"I don't know."

"Better get vanilla," I suggested.

She licked it happily as we drove back to her house. There we found Mr. Nally pacing up and down the driveway. A half-hour seemed to be the maximum time he allowed for visits. Not much time to get acquainted with a small, frightened child, I thought.

The foster mother took Molly inside while Mr. Nally explained his plan for the next day. "I want you to come at the same time tomorrow. That will be easier. The other children will be in school. The foster mother will put Molly's things in your car. You invite her to go for a ride just like you did today. But you won't come back here. You'll take her home. Understand?"

"Yes."

"Good."

"Can we bring our son?" I asked. "He's anxious to come."

"I guess so. Warn him not to reveal your names. We don't want the foster family to know where Molly's going."

"Why is that?"

"Because they have been in touch with the natural mother. We don't want her to know who you are."

Next morning we all awoke early. It was another beautiful fall day. The sun shone brightly and I could hear the faint cry of migrating ducks. "I have to go to the office this morning," John announced at breakfast. "I can't take another full day off from work, but I'll come home early. We can start right after lunch."

"I'll have sandwiches on the table by eleven-thirty. We can leave here at noon."

"I'll stay home to help," Bruce volunteered.

"No. You can stay home, if you do your homework. I don't want you behind in school."

Our timing proved perfect. We arrived at exactly one-thirty. As we drove up, we could see Mr. Nally pacing up and down the driveway. "She's kept all the children home from school," he blurted out angrily. "It looks like a wake in there."

" What do you want us to do?" I asked.

"You distract Molly while I pack her things into the car. Then put her in and drive off quickly."

"All right." Inside, we found both parents and several children standing around Molly. All of them were crying. The foster mother showed me Molly's pink monkey. "Should I throw this away?"

"No. Don't. She needs familiar toys."

The woman nodded. "I'll pack it."

I turned to Molly. She was dressed in clean blue slacks and a warm flowered blouse. Her hair had been caught up in a white ribbon and curled down her back. She looked lovely but confused. I reached down and took her hand. "Come on, Molly, Let's go swing."

"Okay," she answered looking relieved.

As I pushed her swing, I watched John and Mr. Nally load paper bags of clothing into our car. When they finished, John waved to me. He and Bruce climbed into the front seat. They sat waiting for me.

"Would you like some ice cream now?" I asked Molly.

"I'd like that."

I led Molly around the side of the house trying to avoid the foster family. Before we reached the car, her foster mother came to the door.

"Wait," she called, "don't forget her coat." The woman hurried out carrying a shabby blue coat. "Be a good girl and don't cry," she told Molly as she slipped her little arms into the sleeves.

Molly nodded silently.

I answered "thank you." I picked Molly up and put her in the back seat of the car. Hurriedly, I slid in beside her and slammed the door shut. I saw her pink monkey sticking out of the top of a paper bag. I handed it to her. "Here's monkey. He can go for ice cream, too."

Molly smiled and took him into her arms holding him tight. I picked them both up and put them on my lap. Glancing back, I saw the whole foster family on their porch. They stood crying and waving as John gunned the engine and hurriedly sped away.

Molly slept all the way home not awakening until John stopped the car in our driveway. Then she opened her eyes and yawned. John turned around and smiled at her. "Would you like to see our house?"

"All right," she answered sleepily.

John opened the car door for us while Bruce went ahead into the house. "I'm thirsty," he explained. "I'll fix us both something to drink."

"Okay," I answered, just make sure you give Molly one of the small cups. Her hands aren't very big." I turned to Molly. "Are you thirsty?"

She nodded.

John lifted her out of the car so I could get out.I took her hand and led her inside. Bruce put a cup of juice and a cookie in front of a high kitchen chair. "You sit here, Molly."

She put monkey on the table, and climbed into the chair.

Bruce sat next to her. "Hi, Molly, I'm Bruce. When you finish eating I'll take you outdoors to see our swing set."

"Okay."

While Bruce played with Molly, John brought in the paper bags containing her clothing. I opened them in the kitchen. On top I found a baby bottle filled with milk. No one had told me that she still drank from a bottle. I put it in the refrigerator. She might want it at bedtime.

I found a dozen diapers. They seemed clean, until I took them out of the bag. A flea jumped off one.

"I'd better rewash everything," I told John.

"I guess so."

Together we unpacked her clothing putting everything into my washer. She didn't have much, two or three blouses, two pairs of pants, a few underpants and one worn blue coat. When we finished I fixed some spaghetti for our supper. "She should like that." I told John. " Everybody likes spaghetti."

Bruce played outside with Molly until I called them for dinner. When they came in Molly's face was flushed with excitement.

"Did you have fun?" I asked.

"Yes. Bruce can push me high."

"She loves to swing," Bruce said. "But she kept saying that there were fleas in the grass."

"I'm not surprised. I found some in her clean clothes."

"Never mind," John added. "We laundered everything."

"Now it's time to clean up for dinner. Come, Molly," I reached down to take her hand. "I'll show you our bathroom."

"Okay."

After washing her hands, I lifted her into her chair at the dining room table. She sat with her back to a big picture window. She stared at her plate for a minute, then swung around so she could look out that window. It was starting to get dark so instead of seeing outside, she saw all of us reflected in the darkened glass. "Look," she exclaimed, pointing, "I can see you."

"Yes," I answered. "Now turn around and eat your dinner."

"I like to sit this way."

"All right," I handed her a piece of buttered bread. "But you have to eat."

She took the bread.

Molly ate the rest of her meal with her back to us. She put the food into her mouth, then turned around to chew it. Even though dinner went slowly, no one complained. For dessert, I put her ice cream in a cone to make it easier to eat.

After dinner, I helped her prepare for bed. "Come on, Molly," I lifted her down from her chair. "I'll help you undress. You can have a warm bath."

I led her into the bathroom. After starting the bath, I turned to undress her. As soon as she saw the water running, she began to scream. "NO, NO I want to go home."

I tried to calm her. "This is your home now. You live here with us."

Tears poured down her face. "NO! Take me home."

I thought the idea of a bath frightened her, so I shut off the water. I carried her into her bedroom. "Look at this nice soft bed. Wouldn't your monkey like to sleep here?"

She quieted down, thinking about it. "I guess so."

"I'm sure he would. Let's ask him?" I called to John. "Bring monkey up from the dining room. And warm that bottle for her, too."

"Okay," he called back. A moment later he handed me monkey. Carefully, I turned back the blanket and tucked monkey into bed. "See. He likes it here," I told Molly.

Molly nodded slowly and stopped crying.

"I'll put your pajamas on. You can climb in beside him." As I lifted her onto the bed, she reached for monkey, holding him tightly. I undressed her. When I took off her underpants, I saw a line of flea bites around her legs. I'll have to wait until tomorrow to do anything about them, I decided. I put a diaper on her and tucked her into the bed.

John arrived with her milk. "How's that?" he asked giving it to her. She didn't answer. She put the bottle into her mouth and closed her eyes.

"Poor thing, she's exhausted," I told John as we tiptoed away.

Next morning, I awoke to find Molly standing beside my bed holding monkey tightly in her arms. She said nothing, just stood staring at me.

She must be terrified, I thought smiling at her in a reassuring manner. "Good morning, Molly,"

"Can I go home now?"

"No, honey, you're going to live here now. You'll like it, I promise."

Her face clouded and she started to cry . "I want to go home."

"I'm sorry. I can't take you back there. I can fix you some breakfast." I tried to be my most charming as I climbed out of bed. "I bet monkey is hungry. What do you think he would like to eat?"

She looked down at the pink monkey in her arms and shook her head. "I don't know."

"Let's go find something." I took her hand and led her to the kitchen.

When she was seated in the high chair with monkey beside her, I showed her an assortment of individual cereal packages. "You choose one for monkey."

She looked them over carefully, then pointed to one.

"Good." I poured cereal into a bowl. "Does monkey like milk on it?"

"No." She picked up a flake of cereal and put it into her mouth.

"How about milk for you?"

"Okay."

I poured her milk, then turned to put a pot of coffee on the stove. She sat quietly eating while I fixed breakfast for the rest of the family.

She still needed a bath, so after breakfast, I hunted in an old toy box until I found a pair of yellow plastic ducks. "Come on, Molly." I said showing them to her. "Let's see if you can teach these ducks to swim."

"Okay." She followed into the bathroom. I ran water in the tub and handed her the toys. "Here, you put them in."

She nodded. Taking them, she knelt next to the tub. "I can't reach the water. I'm too little."

"You'll have to get in with them. Can you do that?"

For a moment she looked frightened. Then she changed her mind. "I guess so."

"I'll help you undress." I unfastened her pajamas and slid them off. I removed the diaper which she had worn during the night. She stood there holding a duck in each hand.

"Ready?"

"Yes." She raised her arms so I could lift her.

I let her play with the ducks until the water began to get cold. Then I started to wash her. She paid little attention so I decided to wash her hair. "Shut your eyes. I'm going to pour water on your head."

"No!" she cried, suddenly alarmed.

"It's all right." I poured a little water onto the back of her head. "See. It doesn't hurt."

Slowly, I poured water onto the rest of her head and washed her hair with baby shampoo. She sat with her hands clenched and her eyes tightly closed. I worked as quickly as possible. As soon as she was clean I lifted her out and wrapped her in a soft towel. That'll take care of the fleas, I thought. I dried her off and dressed her in fresh clothing. "That wasn't so bad was it?"

"You got soap in my eyes."

"No, I didn't."

"You did so." She started to cry again. "Take me home."

"I'm sorry. I can't do that."

She stamped her foot and set her jaw in a defiant manner. "I want to go home now."

"When your hair dries, I'll take you outside to play on the swing."

"No."

"Okay. You and monkey can play in your room." I brought her monkey up from downstairs along with a box of toys which Bruce had collected. "Here," I said giving them to her. "you can play with these."

Molly played alone most of the day coming out only for meals and a short swing with Bruce. She ate with her back to us using the reflection in the window glass to watch us.

I tucked her into bed that night with a sigh of relief. "It's been a hard day," I told John. "I realize that Molly's frightened and angry. How do we reassure her? I don't know how to convince her that it's all right?"

"That will take time."

"A long time, I'm afraid."

Chapter 15

The next few weeks passed quietly. One day I found Molly standing in the kitchen with her fingers caught in a drawer. She hadn't cried or called out. She just stood there waiting for me to find her. I remembered that her foster mother had told her to "Be a good girl and not cry." But this was ridiculous.

"It's okay to cry when you're hurt," I told her as I opened the drawer.

She just nodded.

On Halloween, I took her tricks-or-treating. We stopped first at our next door neighbor's. He was an executive for an insurance company. His wife, Reba, was a friend of mine. She had no children, just two darling little dogs. When we rang their bell, the man jumped out and shouted "BOO." Molly shrieked in terror and ran home. I didn't blame him. He knew nothing about children. But that ended Molly's Halloween.

A few weeks later, I was busy cleaning when the phone rang. It was Bruce calling from school. His voice sounded heavy with emotion. "I knew you wouldn't have the television turned on, so I called to tell you that President Kennedy has just been shot."

My heart jumped. "Oh my goodness. I'll turn it on right away." I watched the rest of that morning. Bruce joined me as soon as school ended. At first, we didn't realize that the President was dead, but it soon became obvious. Like the rest of the nation, we were shocked and saddened. How could this happen to our popular, young President? Bruce was especially upset. He had lost his sister, his grandfather, and now the President whom he greatly admired. It was a lot for a young man to bear.

A short time later, Mr. Nally, the social worker, came to check on us. He was upset when he saw Molly. "You've cut her hair," he blurted out.

"Yes." I answered. "She cried so hard every time I try to comb it. I thought it would be easier if it were short."

"Oh." He sounded unconvinced. "I guess it will grow out."

"And I hope that then, she'll have stopped fearing me."

The hair grew slowly and with it a kind of truce between us. Molly no longer questioned my decisions. But she didn't trust me either.

Christmas day came and Molly accepted the toys we gave her without interest. She preferred her pink monkey to anything new. The only thing that really excited her was playing in the snow with Bruce. "Come outside, Molly," Bruce said after we'd opened our presents. "I'll build you a snow house."

"Okay." She laughed excitedly as Bruce bundled her into her coat and led her outside. Inky, the black cat, followed them.

A large, ice covered drift of snow had formed behind the house. Bruce started digging into it to form a cave. As Molly watched, Inky dug furiously in the snow beside her. She clapped her hands in delight "Look, Bruce. Inky is making a house for me, too."

From that day on, Inky became her cat. He followed her around all day and slept on her bed at night. I was thankful that they had found each other. They both needed love.

By February, snow lay deep around us. I asked Mr. Nally if we could take Molly to Florida for a two week vacation. I needed his permission. Molly was still a foster child and ward of the state. She wouldn't be legally ours until the probationary period ended and a judge approved the adoption.

"Yes." he agreed, "You can take me with you to supervise," he joked.

"We'd be happy to," I lied.

"My boss won't let me go."

Two weeks later, the whole family flew to Fort Myers, Florida. We rented a car and drove to a cottage on the gulf. It was built on stilts a little way back from the water. Under the porch we found cool, well shaded sand, an ideal place for a young child to play. Molly loved it.

We had three small bedrooms, a living room decorated with pictures of the ocean and an open kitchen with a breakfast bar.

"It has maid service," I told John, "I'm not going to cook, either."

"Not even sandwiches?"

"I'll make those. We can buy rolls and fruit for breakfast. But we're going out for dinner every night."

"Okay," John agreed, "It's your vacation, too."

After unpacking,I put on my swimming suit. Then I dressed Molly in a blue suit with white flowers on it. "Come on, Molly, we'll go swimming."

We walked down to the waters edge. White foam left patterns on the hard packed sand and tiny crabs popped in and out of abandoned shells. As I started into the water, Molly drew back, frightened.

"What's wrong?"

"The fish will eat me."

"No they won't. Fish swim in deep water. I won't take you out that far. We'll walk along the edge. See." I waded in until the water just covered my toes. "That's as far as we'll go."

Molly followed cautiously. As a wave touched her bare feet, she laughed. "It tickles."

Just then Bruce came running down the beach. He and John had been hunting for shells. "Look, Molly," he called, "I've something to show you." He opened his hand. Inside was a tiny hermit crab peeking out of an abandoned shell."You want to hold it?"

"It'll pinch me."

"Maybe, but not hard." Bruce held out the crab so Molly could touch it. "See, it's too small to hurt you."

Cautiously Molly touched the tiny crab. "Now put it back."

Bruce laughed. "All right. I'll go find a something else to show you."

After swimming we showered and dressed for dinner. Our resort had a nice restaurant. Next to it, we found an attractive pool with tables and chairs around it.

"Tomorrow, I'll take you swimming in this pool," I promised Molly.

"I'd like that."

Next morning, we awoke to the sound of a bird singing loudly in a nearby palm tree. John grumbled. "What is that bird? A common Florida squawker?"

I laughed. "No. It's a mocking bird."

"I wish it would shut up! But I'm up, so I'll take Bruce fishing."

Molly and I walked over to the pool. We found a small boy about Molly's age playing on steps which led down into the shallow end of the pool. Nearby, two women sat at a table drinking Bloody Mary's. I gathered that they were the boy's mother and grandmother.

I helped Molly onto the first step and sat next to her. "Hi," I said to the boy. "This is Molly. She's going to swim with you."

"Hi," the boy answered. "Look what I can do." Hanging onto the bottom step, he kicked his legs in the deep water. "See. I can swim."

"Good." I answered. "Just be careful. You might slide off that step."

"I won't."

Cautiously, Molly sat down on the first step. The water just covered her legs and hips. I watched her carefully as she wiggled her toes and splashed happily in the clear water.

Suddenly, I realized that the little boy was no longer on the steps. He had slipped off into deep water. He lay on the bottom of the pool. I reached down and grabbed him swinging him up onto the grass beside the two women. He lay gasping for breath.

"He was in over his head," I told the women. "I think he inhaled water. We'd better get it out of him."

"No," the older woman said. "Leave him alone. You'll frighten him."

"Are you sure?" I asked the other woman.

She nodded. "Leave him alone."

"Okay," I shook my head. "He's your child."

"That's right." The woman took a big gulp of her drink.

"Come on, Mol," I took Molly's hand. "Let's go home."

Next day, when the maid came to clean, she had big news. " There was an ambulance here last night."

"Really, why?" I asked.

"They took a little boy to the hospital. He was really sick He couldn't breathe. A guest told me that he took in water from the pool."

"That's bad. I hope he's all right."

"Yes." The maid agreed.

At that moment Bruce arrived carrying an old mayonnaise jar which he held up. "Look what I caught."

I peered into the glass. "What is it?"

"It's a little lizard which can change colors. I put it on a green leaf and it turned green. When I first found it on a brown fence, it was brown."

The maid saw it and cried out. "Don't let that thing loose in the house. I won't clean here if you do."

"Don't worry, " I assured her, "it can't hurt you. It's just a little chameleon. How did you catch it, Bruce? As a child, I tried to catch them. I always grabbed it by the tail and the tail broke off."

"I distracted it with one hand and slipped the jar over it

with the other. Can I take it home?"

"No. You can't take it out of state. Besides, Wisconsin is too cold."

"All right. Let me show it to Molly. I'll set it free when we leave."

"You'll have to feed it in the meantime."

"I'll catch flies."

"And give it water. You have to drip the water onto it's head. Those little things won't drink out of a bowl."

"Why not?"

"I don't know. My brother had one once when we lived in Florida. That's what he did."

"Okay. I have to go find a red leaf. I want to show Molly what happens when it sits on something red."

"She's playing in the sand under the house. Don't scare her."

"I wouldn't do that." Bruce looked hurt at the thought. "I like Molly. I just want to show it to her."

"Just remember that she's easily frightened."

Bruce nodded and went off to find his leaf. The maid said nothing more. She continued to clean. On the final day of our vacation a strange woman came instead.

"What happened to our regular maid?" I asked her.

"She took her son to the hospital. She let him play with a jelly fish at the beach. It was poisonous."

"That's terrible. I hope he'll be all right."

"So do I."

Later I told John about it.

He shook his head. "What a foolish woman."

"Yes," I agreed. "She was afraid of a harmless chameleon. Then she let her child play with a poisonous jelly fish."

"Thank goodness we know what's dangerous and what isn't."

"And can teach our children the difference."

I turned and called to Bruce. "We're packed. "Time to take the chameleon outside and let it go."

"Okay," he answered. He took Molly by the hand. "Come on Mol, I'll show you how fast this thing can run."

John smiled as they headed out the door. "They get along well."

I nodded. "Thank goodness."

In June, Mr. Nally decided that we had been foster parents long enough. "You can petition the court for permanent custody any time you want," he told John and me.

"I thought we had to wait a full year?" I answered, surprised.

"That's what we tell people. It usually takes that long. But in your case, I have no doubts. I'm sure you will make excellent parents, so go ahead. All the judge needs is my recommendation."

"Thank you," I answered, excited. "We'll do it right away."

Our attorney filed the necessary papers. A court date was set "The judge doesn't want a formal hearing," he told us. "He'll meet you in his chambers. You are to bring Molly with you. He wants to see her."

"But she's so little," I protested.

"I know. He still wants a look at her."

"Okay," I agreed reluctantly.

The meeting was scheduled for one o'clock in the afternoon. That was Molly's nap time. I couldn't change it. I dressed her in a blue, summer dress. She looked lovely. Her hair had grown out quite a bit. I brushed it back and tied it with a bright blue bow.

John drove us to court. I had never been in a courthouse before. I felt very nervous. The brick building was impressive, large with white pillars at each corner and wide steps which had been polished until they shone.

We walked down a long hall which smelled of floor polish and cigarette smoke. Benches alternated with windows on the left side while doors lined the right. Beside each door hung a sign telling us the name of that courtroom's judge. We found the one we wanted about half way down.

John opened the door slowly. I was scared to death. I held Molly's hand and followed John. The room was empty except for the judge who sat in his big chair reading something on his desk   He was dressed in an ordinary business suit, not the black robes which I had expected.

The judge put me at ease. "This is the fun part of being a judge. He smiled as he got up and showed us into his office. He pointed to seats, then pulled his huge, leather chair up behind an immense desk.

He rummaged through a pile of folders while we sat waiting. I lifted Molly up on my lap. She didn't make a sound, just watched every move this strange man made. After a few moments her head began to nod. Her eyes blinked as she fought to stay awake.

"So this is the little girl you want to adopt." The judge smiled at her. He leafed through a bunch of papers. "Everything seems to be in order." Suddenly, his expression changed as he noticed Molly's head nodding and her eyes half closed. "What's wrong with her?"

"It's her nap time," I explained. "She usually sleeps in the afternoon."

The judge looked relieved. "That's right, small children do sleep in the daytime don't they?"

"Yes."

The judge nodded and returned to his papers. "What do you want to call her?"

"Her name's Molly."

"Is that her original name?"

"Yes."

Of course, I thought. What did he think we'd called her all these months? Then I realized that most people adopted new-born babies.

"We usually don't give this to parents," the judge said handing me a piece of paper."But since you know her name, you might as well have it."

"Thank you." I had no idea what he'd given me. Glancing at it, I saw that it was the court order making Molly ours. It showed her last name, which we had not known before, and her date of birth. I tucked the paper into my purse carefully. I didn't want to wake Molly who was now asleep.

The judge continued to talk. "Her birth certificate will be sealed and a new one issued. It will show you as her parents and the new last name which you have given her. The place and time of birth will not change. You can get a copy of her new birth certificate from the bureau of records just like you would for a natural child. Do you understand?"

John and I both nodded.

"Good." He waved toward the door. "That's all you have to do."

"Thank you." John stood up and took Molly from me. "I'll carry her."

"Thanks, again," I called back as we headed out the door.

Chapter 16

In spring of 1964 we decided to take the children to meet their paternal grandmother. A trip to Alaska would be exciting. John was the only one who had ever been there. We would go as soon as Bruce's school let out. "The mosquitoes won't be so bad then," John explained. "It'll still be pretty cold, so they won't be active."

I agreed. I had heard stories about convicts who escaped from Alaskan prisons. They surrendered to police after a couple of days in the wild with those mosquitoes.

We were all excited until Easter week. Bruce was away skiing with his friend Timmy Baak. On Good Friday, a terrible earthquake struck Alaska. Much of Anchorage was ruined. John tried frantically to telephone his mother, but to no avail.

As we sat glued to the television, we heard pounding on the front door. Rushing to open it, John found Dr. Baak carrying Bruce in his arms. On his leg was a large plaster cast. "Bruce broke his leg," Timmy explained. "My Dad put the cast on it."

"Where do you want him?" Dr. Baak asked.

I motioned to the davenport. Doctor. B. put Bruce down as carefully as possible. "Boy, he's heavy!"

"I appreciate your carrying him in," I answered. "Take off your coat. I'll fix you a cup of coffee."

"No, thanks. We've got to get home. Here take these pills." He reached into his pocket and handed me a prescription bottle. "If Bruce has a lot of pain, give him one every four hours."

"I'm in pain now," Bruce cried.

The doctor nodded. " You can give him one now." He turned towards the door. "Let's go Timmy."

"I'm coming," Tim answered. "See you soon." He waved to Bruce as he followed his father outside.

"Bye," Bruce answered.

After several days, John reached his mother by phone. "I'm fine, she assured him. But a lot of septic tanks cracked. We're having trouble getting pure drinking water."

"They'll be fixed by the time we arrive," John assured her " June is still a long time away."

"My leg has to heal first," Bruce added.

"Foolish, wasn't it," I told John that night. "We were worrying about the wrong person."

He nodded. "Worrying is like that. It never accomplishes anything."

"We can't help it. We do it anyway."

"True. Discouraging, isn't it."

Bruce's leg healed slowly. He developed arthritis which caused the leg to swell inside the cast. One Sunday morning he was in so much pain that I called Dr. Baak.

"I'll be right over," he assured me. A moment later he arrived carrying a portable power saw. Bruce's eyes popped when he saw it. "What are you going to do with that?"

"Cut the cast."

"Can I watch," Molly asked following us into the room.

"No, you can't." I answered firmly. "You and I will wait outside."

I led her into her own bedroom. Dr. Baak started the saw. We heard horrible screeching noises as he cut through the plaster. My heart pounded. What if his hand slips and he cuts Bruce's leg off?

I didn't want Molly to sense my fear so I tried to remain calm. "Here's Monkey," I held up her pink toy. "See if he can wear one of your dresses."

"That's silly. My clothes are too big for him."

"He could just wear your tee shirt."

"That will look like a dress on him."

I nodded. "And there will be plenty of room for his tail."

Molly laughed at that. We found a blue shirt. I put it on the monkey. "How's that look?" I yelled over the sound of the saw.

"Good!" she shouted as the noise stopped. "Can I show it to Bruce?"

"In just a minute. Let me make sure they're finished first." I peeked around Bruce's door. Dr. Baak was fitting the back half of the cast to Bruce's leg. "Can we come in now?"

"Yes," the doctor answered. "I'm almost finished."

"It feels better now." Bruce looked pale but relieved. "Come on in."

Molly bounced through the door carrying monkey. "Look, Bruce, monkey is dressed for our trip."

"It will be a while before we go," Bruce answered." My broken leg must heal first."

"That won't take long. By the time school ends, you'll be as good as new." Dr. Baak assured him.

We made our plans carefully. John was anxious to stop in Seattle to see his family and friends. He hadn't been there since 1950. Instead of flying directly from Chicago to Anchorage we flew to Seattle first and then on to Alaska. We planned to visit relatives on the return trip because an overnight on the coast worked out better. We bought first class plane tickets and paid in advance for our hotel in Anchorage. That way Molly wouldn't get too tired. "A thirteen hour flight will be hard on her," I warned John.

"I know. After all she's only three."

The trip went smoothly enough. We were traveling west so the stewardess served us dinner twice on the way to Seattle and again on the flight north to Anchorage. It was ten o'clock at night Alaska time when we arrived. It was still light and the streets were filled with people.

"They act like it's mid- afternoon," Bruce commented.

"People here don't sleep much in summer," John explained.

" They get enough of that in winter when it's dark."

That wasn't true of Molly. It was after midnight our time, much too late for her. She fell asleep in the cab. John carried her into our busy hotel. Searching for a place to put her down, John found an empty sofa in a quiet corner. "You wait here with her while I check in," he told me.

"Okay."

"I'm going with you, Dad," Bruce decided.

They were gone a long time. I was beginning to think about waking Molly up and going to look for them when they finally returned. Bruce was laughing. "We're staying in the presidential suite," he blurted out.

"What?"

"They couldn't find our reservation," John explained. "They had a sign on the wall saying that if you had a reservation and they couldn't accommodate you, they would pay for your room at another hotel. It's lucky I had our confirmation in writing, because they're full. When I showed them our reservation and pointed to the sign, they gave us the presidential suite."

I shook my head in disbelief. "I don't care where we sleep as long as I have a bed under me."

"Let's get upstairs." John picked up Molly and headed for the elevator. There was no one to help with the bags. Bruce and I struggled behind him with our luggage. The presidential suite turned out to be the only rooms on the top floor. Opening the door, we saw a large room with huge windows on two sides and a wet bar on the third. The furnishings included two big, modern sofas decorated in a burnt orange material and a highly polished dining room table. An ornate chandelier hung above it.

Standing in that room, we could see most of Anchorage spread out below. It felt like looking down from an airplane. I was too tired to be impressed. An open door led to the presidential bedroom. It had the biggest bed that I had ever seen. Beyond it was another room with twin beds. John put Molly down in the first room. She hardly moved as I took off her clothes and tucked her in.

"I'll sleep here with her," I whispered to John. "You and Bruce can share the next room."

He nodded. Bruce picked up their suitcases and headed for the door. "Sleep well," he whispered.

I think I was asleep before I hit the bed. I hadn't been that way long when I heard Bruce at my side. "Mom," he whispered, "the President has arrived and wants his room."

"Your dreaming. Go back to bed."

"No. He's in the shower. I heard water running."

"What?" I gasped, suddenly awake.

"It's true."

I searched for my robe and followed Bruce into the next room. I could see light shining under the bathroom door. From its faint glow I could see that both beds were empty. "It's your father, not the President," I told him irritably. "Go back to sleep."

"What's he doing in the shower?"

"I don't know. It's the middle of the night. Go back to sleep."

I climbed into my own bed and fell back to sleep. I was awakened again by John and Bruce talking in the next room. A moment later they arrived at my bedside. Both were fully dressed.

"What time is it?" I asked sleepily.

"It's four in the morning," John answered.

"What are you doing up?"

"I couldn't sleep, so I decided to take a shower. Now Bruce and I are going to go outside and look around."

"In the middle of the night?"

"It's light outside. It doesn't get very dark in Alaska in

summer."

"I want to see the earthquake damage," Bruce explained.

"Me, too," added Molly who was now awake.

"I think you're crazy," I complained.

"It's all right, Molly. You can come," John promised

"I'm going back to sleep." I rolled over and shut my eyes.

The next thing I knew they had returned. "Wake up, Mommy. We're back," Molly cried as she jumped on my bed.

"What time is it?" I mumbled to John.

"About six-thirty. The children are hungry."

"I'm starved," Bruce complained.

"We walked down to the beach and saw a lot of damage down."

"But nothing to eat," Bruce added. "The restaurants were all closed."

"Naturally," I yawned. "It's the middle of the night."

"They open at six-thirty. Hurry and dress. We have just enough time to eat and pack before we leave for the airport."

I groaned.

We had booked an early flight into the interior where John's mother lived. We didn't have much choice. Only three planes a week flew there. We ate a quick breakfast, then headed for the airport.

"Now I want you to be careful when at your grandmother's," John told the children. "You are to stay within sight of the house at all times. Children have been lost in the wilderness and never seen again. You must be especially careful to watch for bears. They can be dangerous."

The children promised, but they weren't prepared for the first bear we saw. A huge stuffed bear stood in the middle of the airport terminal towering over us. It must have been twenty feet tall. Molly took one look at it and turned white. "I don't want to go."

"It's all right," I assured her. "There won't be any bears in your grandmother's house."

"Are you sure?"

"Yes, I'm positive. Bears stay in the woods and we won't go there."

"Okay." She didn't sound convinced.

The plane we boarded proved unusual. It carried both passengers and freight. There were six rows of seats in the middle. In front, were eight large crates each of which contained a dog. A sled team, I guessed.

The back of the plane held lumber and other building materials. There were no cabin attendants, and no rest rooms. The pilot talked directly to us. "Where you folks headed?" he asked as we sat down.

"We're going to Circle Hot Springs to see my mother," John said.

"That's great. You grow up around here?"

"Not around Circle Hot Springs. I was raised in Nome."

"That's mighty cold country."

"Don't I know it!"

"Since it's the children's first time in, I'll give them the scenic tour. You can see a lot from the plane."

"Thanks," Bruce answered excitedly.

The pilot flew slowly above a river. We could see the glaciers and the wildlife on either side. In some places, the ice looked clear blue.In others it seemed old and dirty with huge cracks in it. We saw a mountain goat on the ice. At lower elevations we saw dense forests. We flew for twenty minutes without seeing anything but the tops of trees. There were no roads, no houses, just endless miles of trees. The flight was bumpy. Before long Molly got sick. She looked at the mess she had made and started to cry.

"It's all right," I comforted her. "It's not your fault." I spent the last few minutes of our flight trying to console her and clean her up, no easy task without water.

We landed at a small air strip in the middle of a forest. One narrow road led to a prefabricated building beside the runway. A car was parked next to it. Two people waved frantically as the plane taxied to a stop.

"There she is." John pointed to the woman. "That's your grandmother. The man is your step-grandfather Hugh Stone."

We hurried to meet them. Grandmother Stone gave hugs all around while her husband helped John load our suitcases into the car.

"I'm afraid we're not in very good shape," I apologized. Molly was sick on the plane. There wasn't any water to wash her up."

Mother Stone nodded sympathetically. "There isn't any water here at the airport either. It's been a problem since the earthquake. Many of the septic tanks cracked and leaked into wells. A lot of the water is contaminated. It was a terrible earthquake." She shook her head just thinking about it. Then she smiled. "You don't have to worry. We have water at our house and your hotel has plenty of safe water."

"Good." I lifted Molly into the car. "Where are we going now?"

"To our house. I have dinner waiting for you."

"We're not hungry, just tired."

"Dinner will revive you."

"Mom's a wonderful cook," John added.

We drove along dirt roads through a beautiful virgin forest. The cool air smelled clean and softly scented with evergreen. Soon we came to a clearing with a mobile home in it. Smoke curled from the chimney and birds scratched in a bird feeder beside the door.

"This is it. Everybody out," called Grandfather Stone.

Inside the house smelled of freshly baked bread. "It's sourdough," John explained. " Mom keeps a yeast starter in a crock. She makes all her own bread and pancakes."

"I have to," she explained. "There aren't any grocery stores here."

After I cleaned Molly up, we sat down to a delicious lunch of fresh salmon, huge tomatoes that some neighbor had grown, and wonderful sourdough bread.

Stuffed, we set out to find our hotel. It turned out to be a weather beaten rectangular box set out in the middle of no where. I had misgivings, but our rooms were clean and comfortable. Each bed had a warm down comforter on it. I tucked Molly in. She went right to sleep even though it was still only mid-afternoon. Bruce and John went back to John's mother's house to look at pictures from their gold mining days. I lay down beside Molly and soon fell asleep.

The next day we went salmon fishing in a fast moving stream with milky white water. "It's caused by fine silt from the glaciers," John explained. "Drinking too much of it can upset your stomach. My mother's water comes from a well, so we won't have a problem."

We didn't catch any fish. The salmon we had eaten the day before came from a fish wheel. It caught salmon by throwing them into a water container. Local people were allowed to take a certain number each year for personal use. Grandfather Stone took Bruce down to see it.

Molly and I stayed home. We watched a little squirrel which came to eat at the bird feeder. He had huge eyes which grandmother Stone explained, "The big eyes makes it easier for him to find food during the long Alaskan night." I didn't really believe that, but he was fun to watch.

We went to meet the neighbors. We left at ten in the morning and didn't get back until midnight. We drove two hundred miles to visit four families. One of them fed us a dinner of caribou meat and spaghetti. I came back exhausted.

Finally, we said good-bye. We climbed back on the airplane for the long ride home. After an overnight stop in Seattle so John could see the rest of his family, we boarded a plane for Minneapolis. Molly went to sleep as soon as the plane took off. She slept until we were circling Minneapolis. She ate her breakfast just as the sun set. One more commuter plane carried us home. I had never been so tired. Thank goodness we were home where if got dark at night!

Exhausted from the trip to Alaska, I found it hard to sleep at night. I tossed and turned worrying about the relationship between my husband and my older brother, Sam. When Father died Sam gained control of the company. Now he decided that my husband wasn't doing his share of the work. Sam yelled at me insisting that I change him. John, thought that Sam worked him too hard. He came home at night and bullied me. "He's your brother. Tell him to stop."

"How?" I asked, trying not to cry. "Neither of you listens to me."

"You have to do something."

"I can't."

I lay awake nights trying to think of a way to help. Fatigue turned to exhaustion and then into deep depression. I went to see a psychiatrist. He was no help. "You're spoiled and stubborn," he decided.

I looked for another doctor. There was none available. Christmas made things worse. I kept remembering Jenny. I cried in secret. One bitterly cold day in early January, I started to cry and couldn't stop. I sat down in a living room chair and sobbed myself silly.

"What's wrong?" John asked.

"Nothing." I cried even harder.

"There has to be something."

I shook my head, but continued to wail.

John turned away and called Sam, who hurried over. The two stood staring at me. "Okay, tell us what's wrong?" Sam insisted.

"I can't stop crying," I gasped through my tears.

John called our doctor who prescribed a sedative. Then he called the psychiatrist who arranged for me to go to the Mayo Clinic.

My husband drove me over. At Saint Mary's hospital, a young, blond doctor took one look and admitted me. Once again my feet echoed down those empty halls. I felt dizzy and nauseous as I took the long walk to the psychiatric ward.

John left me there and went home. I wasn't in a locked ward. I could come and go at any time. The trouble was, I didn't want to go anywhere. I just laid in bed and cried.

"I think your problem is grief," my handsome, young doctor said. "You have never grieved properly for your lost daughter."

None of my family wants me to grieve, I thought. They have erased Jenny. They act as though she never existed. I can't do that. The more they distance themselves from her, the harder I hang on to her memory.

I didn't say any of that. "The problem is the friction between my husband and my brother. They're angry at each other and both blame me. I don't know what to do. I don't run the company."

"You can't spend the rest of your life crying."

"Yes, I can." I burst into tears again.

"We'll see." He smiled kindly.

For three weeks, I alternated between crying, sleeping, and trying to work out my problems. Patients were not allowed to spend their days in bed. I had to dress, eat in the dining room and socialize with others.   In addition to private counseling, everyone had to attend group therapy.

Gradually, I realized that I wasn't alone. Other people had troubles, too. I stopped crying and faced the issues. I wanted a hobby for myself. I also needed to encourage my husband to leave the family business. That company had belonged to Father. We were still living with his ambitions, in his shadow, the shadow of Gray Tower. I had to find a way to get away from that.

Feeling better with goals in mind, I called John to pick me up. It was almost Valentines day. While I waited for John, I walked across the street to a drug store. I bought Valentines for Molly, Bruce and John. It was the first time I had been shopping in a month.

Spring came at last. The sun shown. Fields bloomed with masses of brilliant, yellow flowers. I bloomed, too.I decided upon a hobby. I would build a trout pond. My father had always wanted a private lake. He had never found one.

In Wisconsin, it was impossible to own a lake. You can buy the land around it, but not water. That belonged to the state. It had to be available to everyone. The exception was an artificial pond. If you built it, you owned it.

"I want some cheap land with springs on it which I can dig out to make a small lake," I told the real estate agent. He was an elderly man with a weathered face which made me think of a retired farmer. He nodded and went to work. Soon he called to say that he had just the thing. "It's perfect," he assured me. "Forty acres with a trout stream and seepage springs coming up through rotten granite. That'll give you a nice, clean bottom."

I nodded. "Trout like a clear lake. My husband and I will drive out and take a look."

"Good. I'll give you written directions. You won't have

any trouble finding it. It's not far."

On Saturday, John and I put the children in our car and set off. The agent was right. We found it easily. The land fronted on a good road with electricity available. Driving up to the gate, we saw rolling fields with a tiny trout stream wandering through them.

Up hill, were acres of scrubby trees mixed with a few evergreens. A herd of young cattle and several worn out horses wandered around nibbling grass. There was no real house, just a funny, old shack on skids which had once been pulled into the forests during lumbering. Next to it stood a new chicken coop and an outhouse. "Let's explore the shack," Bruce said as he jumped out of the car.

"No, you don't," John cried. "I have to check it out first."

"Okay," Bruce grumbled. " Come , Molly, we'll go explore the creek."

John and I went up to the shack and peered inside. We saw a filthy, unmade bed, a table with dirty dishes on it and a desk covered with bills.

"What's all this?" John asked.

"The real estate agent told me about it," I explained. The man who lived here was incompetent. He mortgaged his land to get money to build a chicken coop. But he didn't feed the chickens. They died. The state took him away to a home. Now the bank has foreclosed the mortgage. That's why it's so cheap."

"What about the cows and horses?"

"They belong to a neighbor. This man told someone in a bar that he could put heifers and horses in here for the summer. If we buy the land, we'll be stuck with them until frost."

"On somebody's word?"

"The agent told me oral contracts are binding in Wisconsin."

"It doesn't matter. You aren't in any hurry to dig are you?"

"No. The children can have a lot of fun here in the mean-time."

It smelled bad in the shack. We hurried outside, making sure the door was closed tightly.

Bruce ran over. "Guess what we found? A mouse made a nest out of toilet paper in the outhouse."

I laughed. "That's all right. He can't do any harm."

Suddenly, Molly screamed. I turned and saw her sitting on a fallen log with bees all around her. John started to run. He swooped her up in his arms and kept running as fast as he could. The bees didn't follow. John stopped at a safe distance and put Molly down. "Are you all right?"

"Yes, Daddy. But the bees scared me."

"Those bees must live in that hollow log. You sat on their home."

Molly laughed at that. "I must seem like a giant to them."

"Yes, but from now on, stay away from that log."

"We'll all stay away from it," Bruce said as he came up beside them.

"Good idea. But it's time to go home." They hurried back to me and we all climbed into the car.

"Are you going to buy this place?" Bruce asked.

"Yes," I answered. "But I'll try to get rid of the shack."

"And the bees," Molly added.

After I bought the land, we spent time there. I would pack up the children and a sack full of peanut butter sandwiches. Then we'd drive out to our forty. One night, we even camped overnight. I bought some cots and sleeping bags. Bruce, Molly and I cleaned the chicken coop. "It's not very dirty," Bruce commented as he swept the floor.

"I know," I agreed. "Those chickens must not have lasted long."

"He probably ate them."

"They were supposed to be laying hens."

"There aren't any roosts or nests. Nothing for them to sit on."

"You're right. It doesn't look like chickens were ever in here."

"Maybe there weren't any chickens."

I shook my head. "We'll never know. But there will be chicken here tonight. I asked your father to bring out a cooked one for our supper."

I had brought fruit salad and soda in a cooler. Bruce and Molly picked raspberries from our bushes. "Don't go far," I warned . "Our neighbor told me that there's a bear living back in the woods. Bears like berries, too. So be careful."

"It's okay, Mom." Molly answered. "I'm not afraid of bears any more."

"That's good, but stay close to Bruce anyway."

Our dinner tasted delicious. It was a hot night, so cold food was welcome. After dinner, I sat in a chair listening to night birds and watching stars appear. I took Molly up on my lap to point out the big dipper. As we watched, a shooting star flashed across the sky. "Make a wish," I told her.

"What should I wish for?"

"Anything you want."

She thought for a moment, then nodded keeping the secret to herself.

As soon as it was dark, we rolled our sleeping bags out onto cots and tried unsuccessfully to sleep. The cots felt hard and the building stuffy. "This is just like an unsuccessful slumber party," John grumbled. "I wish I were home in my own bed."

"Me, too," Bruce agreed.

Eventually morning came and we went home. That was the last time we tried to sleep out. When fall came, the farmer took his livestock away. I hired someone to build the pond.

The State Conservation Department designed it for me. We cleared the land using the surplus rotten granite to build a road. The hole was about two hundred feet long by one hundred fifty feet wide and seven feet deep. Winter snow filled it quickly. "It will be beautiful in spring," I told John. "Everything is going well."

"I'm glad, he answered. "I wish things were going better for me. Your brother, Sam, is giving me a hard time. He claims I'm not working hard enough. He says we don't deserve a vacation next summer."

"Why not?" I asked shaking my head.

"He said that we took a vacation before I had worked for the company a whole year."

"We took it when Father told us to," I answered. "He told us to go to the cottage in Michigan so we went. He decided where and when. It wasn't really our vacation at all. More like a command performance."

"I know. That doesn't matter to Sam. There's another problem, too. The city wants to spray all the Elm trees with a pesticide called DDT. They say it will prevent Dutch Elm disease."

"That's terrible. There's an Elm right next to Bruce's school."

"What can we do?"

"I'll go to the town council meetings and try to talk them out of it." I went to the meeting and pleaded unsuccessfully. The man who promoted DDT lived in Madison where it had already been banned, but even pointing that out to the council did no good. My heart sank when they voted to spray.

"We'll have to move," I told John.

He agreed. "I'll need to find another job."

"We can contact an executive placement agency. They'll find you one." John found an agency with a good reputation. They were supposed to find John a job which suited his personality and skills. We paid them a thousand dollars. They mailed John a battery of tests. Then they asked both of us to come to Milwaukee for a personal interview.

I called Neil, the pilot who had flown me to Mayo and to Michigan. "It's a business trip," I told him. "I'll have to find a baby-sitter for Molly."

"Bring her with you. I'll watch her while you're in the meeting."

"She's awfully little."

"That's okay. I like children."

I remembered how good he'd been to Bruce when he flew us to Michigan. "Fine, thank you."

He seemed older now with deep furrows in his brow. He grinned when he saw me. "At last, I get to fly you someplace when it's not an emergency."

"Yes. Finally."

I had dressed in my best suit. A peach knit chemise with a matching satin trimmed jacket over it. John wore his best blue suit and a red tie.

"You certainly look the part," the interviewer told us as he motioned us into his office.

We had left Neil at the airport with Molly. He planned to fly somewhere with her to look at a plane. He would return for us in a couple of hours. The interviewer looked solemn in a charcoal gray suit. He talked to us about our ambitions, our goals, and about which parts of the country we wanted to live in. He asked me if I could do company entertaining. He reviewed John's present work load, title and salary. At the end he said, "we can place you, but you're earning more than your present job is worth. You'll have to take a cut in salary."

John was furious. He stormed out of the office slamming the door. I stayed behind staring at the interviewer not knowing what to say.

"We'll be in touch," he assured me opening the door.

I found John at the end of the hall. He followed me into a cab where his anger burst out. "That man was an idiot. I don't believe a word he said."

"He's not the only one involved. It's the agency that's going to find you a job. Let's wait and see what's offered."

At the airport we found Neil huffing and puffing as he chased Molly up the down escalator. "Have a good meeting?" he asked cheerfully.

John just glowered at him.

"It was indecisive," I answered still hoping good would come of it.

By February, snow lay deep upon our forty obliterating the pond. At home huge envelopes containing job descriptions lay unopened on my desk. John refused to look at them even though the relationship between he and my brother was worse. Sam insisted that every week John drive a hundred miles to our other office and report to Sam directly. The roads were icy. I was sick with worry. "What shall we do?" I asked John.

"I've always wanted to write," John answered. "I could do that."

"I'll tell you what. I'll add up our bills and my outside income. If there's enough money, you can try it for a year."

"Sounds good, but I'm not happy staying here. We still have to worry about the DDT spraying."

"We could move to California. That's where my brother, Don, lives."

"Let's do it."

John quit his job. I started to pack. Then one day the phone rang. It was our neighbor, Reba, the wife of the attorney who had frightened Molly so badly on her first Halloween. "Was your daughter, Jenny, ever exposed to insect repellents?" she asked.

The mention of Jenny brought tears to my eyes. "Yes. Why?"

"My husband just defended a case in which three families sued the manufacturer of an insect repellent. They blamed it for the deaths of their children from aplastic anemia."

"I'm sorry."

"He thought their illnesses sounded much like your daughter's. He recommended that the product be removed from the market. It's no longer for sale. We thought you'd like to know."

"Yes. I'm glad. Thank you for telling me."

That's good news, I thought. Jenny's life served a purpose after all. Other children will live because our neighbor knew her.

I drove out to the forty on a cold February morning. Snow lay deep upon my land. I could see tracks where deer had rounded the pond, but now nothing moved. I said a silent farewell. In my heart, I knew I would never see it again. On the way home, I drove by the cemetery and whispered good-bye to Jenny.

The bags were packed. We took nothing but our clothes, the children and their cats. Snook was old now and terribly frightened of cars. I considered putting her to sleep. Our veterinarian talked me out of it. "That would be too hard on your children. They'll have a difficult enough time leaving home without giving up their pet."

"You're right. What can I do?"

"I'll give you some pills to quiet her. She should be fine."

We left the furniture. It could wait until spring. On a cold, clear morning in late February, we locked our door and started for California.

Epilogue

Janie never returned to the Midwest. Friends wrote to tell her that the Elm trees were sprayed with DDT and that hundreds of song birds died. Her forty was sold to a man who planned to build a retirement home on it and raise hunting dogs. Years later, after their mother died, Sam mailed Janie's portrait to her. It's all that remains of life at Gray Tower.

Biography

Nancy W. Collins spent twenty six years in rural Minnesota and Wisconsin before moving her family to California in 1967. After raising her children, she returned to college. She received a Bachelor of Arts degree with a major in Communication from the University of California at San Diego in 1982. Since then she has published numerous human interest stories in newspapers, several children's articles and three desktop books. She lives with a Yorkshire Terrier named Tina in rural, Northwestern California. In addition to writing, she gardens, participates in wild bird counts, and spoils her grandchildren.